To Sue—
Me? Be nice?
BUAHAHAHAHA!

JC Logan

The Raven Queen

J.C. Logan

For the students of
Waterbury Public Schools

Chapter One

Black Bear's Decision, 1862

The morning sun crested the foothills to the east. It would be a warm day but the brightening sky did little to remove the chill from Caleb Mason's bones. His breath frosted the Pennsylvania air, rising into the sky before being dispersed by the gentle breeze. That breeze felt cool on his skin and raised gooseflesh on his arms.

He looked at the men and boys standing to his right and to his left. Some hung their head, others looked to the sky and whispered useless prayers. A few of them breathed so quickly they resembled a steam engine. Their fear was as palpable as the sweat which covered his forehead. These men thought they had a good idea of what was about to happen. Caleb was fairly certain only a handful of the officers knew the truth of their situation.

He had not intended to eavesdrop. The previous night he was unable to sleep. He walked the camp, past the men sleeping fitfully and the ones on guard duty. Those who were awake regarded him with pity or else averted their eyes. None spoke. At the time he was unsure if perhaps these men simply did not like him. At fourteen years he was the youngest among them. Did they doubt his nerve in battle? Maybe, but that was not it. A pall hung over the camp last night. Every man, it seemed, knew the outcome of tomorrow's battle as if they had already experienced it. Yet they did not flee. Caleb felt proud of them, proud of himself, he supposed, in some small way.   Even the moments when he considered sneaking away, brief as they were, he stood fast. If tomorrow would truly be the last day for these men, it would be for him, as well. He owed it to them. He owed it to his family. And to himself.

The air was not as thick with the sense of despair as it was now, but it was present nonetheless. These men, soldiers and farmers and blacksmiths, men who had fought bravely and with honor since before Caleb joined them, were afraid. It was seeing fear in their eyes that made Caleb's heart beat a little faster.

As he walked the camp he passed by Colonel Williamson's tent. The men inside probably tried to keep their voices low but to Caleb, they may as well have been shouting. The news was not good. The Confederates had pushed their way north with surprising ease. They were camped not more than seven miles distant, and they were many. One of the officers stated the Confederates held a three-to-one advantage in both infantry and cavalry. Another advocated for retreat.   Colonel Williamson scoffed and stated they would stand their ground and meet the enemy. Caleb, never before privy to an officers' meeting, hid in the shadows when they filed out of the colonel's tent. Most looked resigned to death.

Caleb did not sleep the rest of the night. He sat by a fire and counted his ammunition and powder bags. He considered writing a letter to his mother back home in Waterbury, Connecticut. But what was the point? The messengers had been dispatched earlier that evening and were unlikely to return before the battle started. So he sat at the base of a large oak and looked at the night sky and thought of his mother and sisters.

Now he looked at the men standing beside him. One in particular caught his eye. He was older than most and the only man in the regiment who did not seem to regard Caleb with open suspicion. His name was Black Bear. If Caleb could be said to have a friend among these men, it would be this strange man from somewhere out west.

Black Bear's appearance, his demeanor, his prowess in battle, all had fascinated Caleb. The boy asked endless questions whenever he found himself without duties to perform. Black Bear humored him, probably because no one else was willing to speak to him. The men of the regiment regarded him with open suspicion and even fear. As had Caleb at first.

The Indian warrior was tall and muscular. His arms and chest were covered with scars. A rather large pouch was slung over his shoulder and its contents were the source of much speculation among the men. They also

3

kept a close watch on the two hatchets he wore tucked into his belt. In Caleb's brief time with the regiment he had never seen Black Bear so much as touch a rifle. When battle came it was upon his hatchets he relied.

But what most eyes were drawn to, what kept the men around him clutching their rifles and swords, was the object tucked into the back of Black Bear's belt. The first time Caleb had seen it, he stared at it and took a few steps back from the big man. It was an enormous bear claw. The story was that Black Bear had taken it from a very large animal that had attacked him when he was just a boy. Some of the men believed he was no more than five or six years-old when this occurred. Some said the boy was unarmed and took down the bear with sheer savagery. One thing all the stories and opinions agreed upon was that Black Bear was not to be trifled with under any circumstances. Caleb agreed.

Black Bear's expression was not one of fear, as it was with the other men around them. His eyes were narrow and focused on the tree line before them. His hands rested on the handles of his hatchets, his breathing was slow and measured. *This is a true warrior*, Caleb thought for the fifth or sixth time since he first saw Black Bear. *I wish I were as brave*.

A horn sounded in the distance. It cut through the morning air like a blade. Several men took an instinctive step back. Those who were praying ceased their prayers and clutched their rifles a bit tighter. Caleb shifted his feet and glanced in Black Bear's direction. Black Bear remained motionless as ever, his eyes fixed straight ahead.

When the Confederates came, the battle did not go as Caleb or Colonel Williamson envisioned. For one thing, the enemy's numbers were not overwhelming. They appeared made up of mostly militia with a smattering of junior officers leading the charge. Casualties were high on both sides but the Unionists held their ground. Caleb stood his ground and fired his rifle three times. Two had missed hitting anyone; the third and final shot struck a militiaman's shoulder. The impact spun the man as if by an invisible dance partner. He staggered back and was lost in the smoke and noise of the battle.

"Is that it? Did we beat them?" Caleb asked as the Confederates retreated back the way they had come.

"Perhaps," Black Bear replied.

But they had not. The morning mist and the smoke from the guns had thinned considerably and now Caleb could see movement along the tree line roughly two hundred feet from where he stood. The bulk of the Confederate regiment, in numbers even greater than the colonel's estimate, emerged from the darkness of the woods.

"Load!" Colonel Williamson shouted.

The men fidgeted at first but their commanding officer's order cut through their fear. They commenced reloading their rifles.

This time the battle went more as Caleb thought it would. The Confederates came in waves that seemed endless. The Union soldiers fell in droves, Colonel Williamson among them. Caleb did as he could but he was one boy and the enemy was relentless. As the Union line collapsed into total disarray, Black Bear took a blast of buckshot to his left shoulder. The big Indian spun from the impact and dropped the hatchet. Blood trickled down his arm. Caleb gasped. If a mighty warrior such as Black Bear could be felled...

But he did not fall. He seemed to take a moment to collect himself. Then he grabbed Caleb and ran for the top of the hill behind them.

"We're going to die," Caleb said. He was surprised by the flat tone of his voice. He was not frightened; he simply stated the inevitable.

"Cover me," Black Bear barked.

He dropped the bag slung over his shoulder and rooted through its contents. He grunted against the pain in his shoulder and seemed to teeter on the brink of unconsciousness. Caleb looked back over his shoulder. His regiment was gone. Many men lay upon the ground while the few who still lived ran in every direction. The

Confederates gave chase and fired their rifles at them. Caleb licked his lips. His turn was about to come.

Black Bear pulled a small black object from his bag. Caleb did not know what it was but it was carved into a monstrous shape. Something about the idol sent fresh shivers up his spine. Black Bear whispered words that Caleb could not understand.

The boy glanced down the hill. One hundred or so Confederate soldiers charged toward the two of them, shouting and cursing. Caleb clutched his rifle to his chest. This was it.

Something very large surged past him. It took a moment for Caleb to realize it was Black Bear. The warrior hurled himself at the enemy soldiers. Covering his right hand was the giant bear claw. Caleb watched with awful fascination as the Indian crashed into the wall of gray uniforms. Some of the men screamed, several rifle shots rang out. Cutting through the chaotic noise was the scream of a mighty warrior falling before his foes.

That was when something cold and black erupted from the ground. The force of it knocked Caleb off his feet as swiftly as it knocked the air from his lungs. His rifle flew from his hands and was lost. Caleb heard the enemy soldiers gasp and shout. Several more rifles fired at once. When he looked at the enemy, he saw they no longer aimed their rifles at him. Something stood between him and them. It was a zone of darkness but something even darker moved within it, moved in the direction of the Confederate soldiers.

Then Caleb knew no more.

Chapter Two

The Sullivans, 1914

Shawn Sullivan was twelve years-old and he doubted he would see thirteen.

His life had been anything but typical until now. He had lived in Belfast with his father, mother, and younger sister, Maureen. His father's brother, Shawn's Uncle Richard, had telegrammed that America was everything he thought it would be. Jobs were plentiful and there was a lot of money to be made. Uncle Richard had lived there only two years but he already owned a house and was contemplating purchasing an automobile. "If there's that kind of money there, we have to go," Shawn's father had told his mother. And so the Sullivan family packed their bags and boarded an ocean liner for the new world.

Unfortunately, the ocean liner was the *Titanic*. Shawn, his mother and sister found their way into a lifeboat but his father was not as lucky. The last time Shawn saw him, he was standing by the rail watching his family lowered down the side of the sinking ship. Shawn remembered his father's expression. It was sad but there was a hint of something else there, as well. Shawn could not have identified what it was at the time but he figured it out eventually. *Relief*. His father, even knowing he would not make it, was relieved his family would survive.

And they had. Rescued by another ship and brought to New York City, Uncle Richard awaited them on the pier. He brought them to his house in the Bronx and there they lived for a while. One year almost to the day they arrived in New York, the family was on a train heading west.

"Pennsylvania," Uncle Richard told them. He had gotten a foreman job at one of the steel mills that paid even more than he was making in New York. And even better, he had already bought a house only one hour's walk from the factory. This was where they would live.

Shawn had been excited at the time. His excitement waned, however, when he saw the house. It sat atop a hill like the world's largest gravestone. It was painted gray, which matched the sky that day. The grounds were spacious and trees followed the property line as far as Shawn could see. It should have been beautiful. He should have been thrilled to live in a house such as this. All he felt was dread.

It started for him the night Maureen climbed into his bed. She was shaking and her cheeks were wet with tears. Shawn, groggy and not a little upset that he had been woken up, asked, "Whasamatter?" Maureen cried and hugged him tightly. With one hand she pointed to the bedroom door.

Something stood in the doorway. It was big, far too big to be Uncle Richard. It was silhouetted against the hallway electric light, which their mother kept on all night so Maureen wouldn't be afraid of the dark. It looked like a man, albeit one with long hair. And there was something wrong with his right arm. It was larger than his left and its fingers seemed to end in claws.

Any thoughts of being the brave big brother flew from Shawn's head. He screamed. Maureen covered her ears and screamed, too. Shawn looked away, holding his sister so tight neither of them could draw a deep breath. When he looked up again his mother and Uncle Richard were running into the room. The thing in the doorway was gone.

But it did not stay gone. Over the next several weeks he and Maureen saw the thing on more than a few occasions. Shawn never got a good look at it; it always seemed to stay in the shadows, or maybe it generated the darkness itself. He got the impression the man—if it was a man—wore strange-looking leggings and no shirt. And Shawn's eyes were always drawn to the man's right arm, the one that ended in a giant, meaty paw. Its claws often gleamed in whatever meager light reached the thing.

And worse, it was not alone. The birds started showing up outside the house. He could hear them. The first time he scrounged up the courage to peek out his window. The trees that bordered the yard were full of black birds. They cawed and cackled and growled their dirges. Two times after that there were even a few who perched themselves directly outside his window. They did

11

not fly away when Shawn looked their way. One time he threw a book at the window hard enough to chip the glass. The birds held their ground. Shawn did not try to drive them away after that.

And sometimes Shawn saw a woman. He thought it was a woman, despite being able to see no details of the figure. This one was even darker than the man-animal. Except for her eyes. They were such a bright red they nearly glowed. As scared as he was of the man and the oddly-brave black birds, the woman was much worse. Maureen saw them, too. She was just as frightened as was he, but she rarely spoke of them. She walked around the house with her doll clutched to her chest and humming to herself.

Shortly after the woman-thing made her presence known, life in the house deteriorated very quickly. Uncle Richard, to this point loving and supportive of his adopted family, became distant, and then outright hostile. He spent long hours cleaning his hunting rifle. He would take the thing apart, clean every individual piece, place it atop the fireplace mantle, then take it down ten minutes later and start again. Their mother spent much of her time in her rocking chair. First she sewed new clothes for them, but eventually she stopped sewing and simply rocked back and forth and stared out the window. Every so often she would wince and cover her ears as if she had heard a loud noise, although the house was quiet.

12

Then, just last week, Shawn saw his first soldier. The man's coat and trousers were as gray as the outside of the house. He carried a rifle and appeared to be hunting someone in the front yard. When he saw Shawn the soldier swung the rifle in the boy's direction. Shawn saw the muzzle flash but he heard no shot. He was also unharmed. When he opened his eyes the soldier was gone. Shawn hid in his room the rest of that day.

He tried to tell his mother about the strange people in the house only once. She did not react as he had expected. Tears filled his mother's eyes but she said nothing. She continued to stare out the window.

Now, Shawn sat on his bed, Maureen next to him. The door was closed and he had managed through great effort to slide his dresser in front of it. A great deal of noise was occurring downstairs. He heard shouts and things breaking. With every new noise Maureen buried her head a little deeper in his chest. The poor girl was sobbing and every few moments she would let out a sharp cry. Shawn held her close to him.

Footsteps coming up the stairs quite quickly. A banging on his bedroom door. "Shawn! Maureen!" It was their mother.

Shawn's first thought was to run to the door. He could probably muscle the dresser aside if he gave it everything he had. He started to move but his sister wrapped her arms around him more tightly and made him grunt. "It's mommy! I have to let her in!"

"No," Maureen sobbed. "Don't open the door, Shawn."

He tried again to free himself from her but her grip felt like that of an iron vice.

"Stay in there, children," their mother called from the other side of the door. "Don't come out no matter what you hear!"

"Mommy!" Shawn tried for the door again but he could not escape his sister's grip.

Then, silence. The sounds of crashing and breaking things from downstairs ceased suddenly. Their mother, if she remained just outside the room, had also gone quiet.

Footsteps coming up the stairs again. The pace was slow, deliberate. Each one was loud, like the banging of a huge drum. Was it Uncle Richard? No, Shawn did not think so. Whatever this was it could not be human.

Faintly, so softly Shawn could barely hear it, his mother's voice. "Please."

A loud *thud*. A shrill scream that ended abruptly. The sound of something limp and wet hitting the floor. More silence.

Maureen whimpered. "Mommy."

Shawn swallowed. His eyes darted about the room. They settled on the window. "Maureen, come on." He expected her to resist but she did not. If anything, she was a little too complacent in her move to obey him. There was no life to her movements, no purpose. She let go of her brother, accepted his hand when he offered it, and followed him to the window.

Shawn looked outside. The birds were loud tonight, louder than they had ever been. He could not see them; could, in fact, see nothing but darkness. Even the moonlight was denied them. He knew it was a good fifteen feet from his bedroom window to the ground below. Way too far but he saw no other way. He turned back to Maureen. "I'll go first. Then it's your turn, okay? I'll catch you. We're going to be okay, Maureen." Shawn opened the window. A warm August breeze washed over him and chilled the sweat that coated his face and neck. The bird sounds increased in volume until Maureen raised her hands to her ears.

Shawn had one leg out the window when his bedroom door and the heavy dresser in front of it exploded. Wood splinters pelted him and drew blood. Shawn shielded his eyes. Before he did he saw his sister had managed to throw his blanket up in front of her. It billowed with numerous impacts but Maureen appeared unharmed. Shawn turned toward the remains of his bedroom door.

The shadow woman with the red eyes stood in the doorway. Thick black smoke seemed to radiate from her.

It quickly overpowered the electric light in the hall, plunging his bedroom into complete darkness.

"Children," the woman-thing said.

Someone screamed. Shawn, to his horror, realized the scream was coming from him.

Chapter Three

Mr. Bisaillon's 8th Grade Class, Now

Xavier Valsaint was feeling pretty good about himself. Not only was this the best field trip of which he had ever taken part, but he killed it when their guide at the science center asked what he must have thought were pretty tough questions. Xavier knew the answers, all of them. Okay, he guessed on one of them, and he did let Nevaeh answer one just so he wouldn't get picked on when they boarded the bus back to James Buchanan Middle School. But still, it was a good day. He especially liked how Mr. Bisaillon nodded his approval every time Xavier's hand went up. "This kid should be on *Jeopardy!*" their guide suggested after the fourth or fifth correct reply. This was answered with agreement by the teacher and grumbles from the rest of the class, especially from Kyle Reed. Xavier knew he would likely have to answer to Kyle later. The class bully was too focused on him for there to be no repercussions. But for now, he was going to be happy.

He should have texted his mother as soon as the class exited the museum. He had intended to, but as Kyle walked past he brushed Xavier with his shoulder and made the boy drop his *Avengers* backpack. Xavier was aggravated and all thoughts of calling his mom vanished. He didn't say anything to Kyle, who waited at the bus door as if daring Xavier to open his mouth. Xavier simply picked up his backpack and boarded the bus, careful not to bump into the larger boy. He took a seat next to Carlos and hoped Kyle would pick one far away. As it turned out, the class bully chose a seat at the very back of the bus, glaring another kid out of it. So for the trip home, at least, Xavier might be in the clear.

But he still hadn't called his mother. And now it was too late. The bus had left all signs of civilization behind and they were now in what his Uncle Marcus termed "the sticks." Forests thick with trees lined both sides of the two-lane road upon which the school bus travelled. Occasionally an open field would pop up on either side of the road but those were few and far between. His cell read NO SERVICE every time he tried it. That was okay. He would rather tell his mom in person and watch her expression of pride with his own eyes instead of imagining it over a text.

Carlos didn't have much to say and that was just fine. Xavier didn't feel much like talking, either. The school year was almost finished, would, in fact, be over already if they hadn't had so many snow days this year. Xavier had enjoyed those snow days, each and every one of them, but now he was paying the piper. Days off in December and January meant more school days in June. Even this didn't get him down, so pleased was he by his performance at the museum. They had nine more days to go and then the summer was his.

The bus rumbled along the country road all by itself. Now that he thought about it, Xavier couldn't remember seeing even one car since the buildings and houses gave way to trees. It made him think of the video games his older brother played. Luke always seemed to favor the games that dealt with the end of the world. He would sit on the edge of his bed and shoot zombies and blow up old cars. Whenever Xavier asked to play, it was always, "You're too young," or, if Luke was having a tough time in the game, "Get out of my face!" There were no zombies out here, and no old, rusted cars by the side of the road. Just trees. Xavier was starting to miss the city.

The bus jolted. Several kids gasped, a couple let out a short, piercing scream, most braced their arms against the seat in front of them. Xavier leaned into the aisle and looked forward. A jet of what appeared to be white smoke was blasting the windshield. The bus driver, a portly woman with her short brown hair pulled back in a tight bun atop her head, swore loudly and piloted the bus to the side of the road. Several kids laughed aloud at the woman's choice of vocabulary.

The bus came to a stop. The white smoke continued to rise from somewhere outside the front of the bus. "Radiator," Xavier heard the driver say. She opened the door and exited the bus.

Mr. Bisaillon stood and held up both hands. "Calm down, boys and girls, calm down. It's okay. There's a problem with the bus. Just stay seated and we'll all be fine."

Kids began whispering to each other. Some laughed, some looked not quite scared but certainly concerned. Xavier was one of them. He didn't know much about automotive technology, but he knew the radiator was serious business. A busted radiator meant they weren't going anywhere. Mr. Bisaillon did not appear worried. He stood at the front of the bus, alternating his gaze from the students to outside the window. Xavier would give anything to see what the bus driver was doing but he knew better than to leave his seat. So he sat and looked out the window and tried not to think about all that white smoke outside.

After several moments the bus driver came back inside. She sat in her seat and Mr. Bisaillon leaned down to speak with her. Xavier watched them intently. He couldn't hear a word they were saying but their body language confirmed his fears. There was something very wrong with the bus and they were likely not going anywhere anytime soon.

Finally, Mr. Bisaillon stood and regarded the students. "All right, listen up. I said listen up. Be quiet in the back! We have a small problem here. There's a mechanical issue with the bus. The driver is calling her dispatcher. I want everyone to remain in their seats. You can speak quietly to one another but I don't want to hear any shouting. If the noise level rises too much you'll have to sit there quietly."

Great, Xavier thought, *stuck in the middle of nowhere with Kyle Reed*. It would only be a matter of time before his nemesis got it into his head to sit behind Xavier and start the tormenting. Mr. Bisaillon and the bus driver were too occupied up front to notice when that happened. Xavier gripped his backpack a little tighter and hoped the bigger boy wouldn't decide that now was a good time for some schoolyard justice.

Mr. Bisaillon stood again and said, "If you have a cell phone please get it out and see if you have service."

"What's the matter?" Nevaeh asked.

"The matter is the radio can't get a signal out here," the bus driver grumbled without turning in her seat. She let fly a few more curse words, causing most of the kids to laugh. Mr. Bisaillon threw her a sour look but the woman seemed not to notice.

"We're stuck?" Carlos asked. His voice cracked at the end.

"We're perfectly safe," Mr. Bisaillon replied. "Just check your cells, please."

Several kids did so, Xavier included. The top left corner of his iPhone still read NO SERVICE. He looked at Mr. Bisaillon and shook his head. No one else had better luck. After several moments during which his students reported they had no signal, Mr. Bisaillon conferred again with the bus driver. Xavier wished he could hear what they were saying but he could not, even when their voices rose above a whisper.

Finally, Mr. Bisaillon stood again and said, "There was a house about a mile and a half back. I'm going to go there and see if I can use their phone. I want everyone to behave responsibly while I'm gone. Mrs. Darby is in charge. If I hear about any issues when I get back you'll be getting homework every night for the rest of the school year."

The noise level on the bus skyrocketed. Mr. Bisaillon spoke with the bus driver again. She seemed less than thrilled to be left in charge of the class. Their conversation was again animated but still Xavier couldn't hear a word. He glanced back at Kyle Reed. The boy was staring at him and smiling. His eyes conveyed what was on his mind: *As soon as Bisaillon's off this bus, you are* mine. Xavier raised his hand.

Mr. Bisaillon looked up and saw him. "Yes, Xavier?"

"Can I come?"

The question seemed to set off most of the kids on the bus. Several more hands shot into the air and many voices repeated Xavier's question. Xavier kept his hand raised. He resisted the urge to look back to see if Kyle mimicked him.

After several moments of noise and waving arms, Mr. Bisaillon quieted the bus. "I don't suppose it'll hurt," he said to Mrs. Darby.

"And less for me to deal with," she replied.

"Fewer."

"What?"

"Nevermind." Mr. Bisaillon looked at his class. "Xavier, Carlos, Nevaeh, Andy and Maya, you can come with me."

More noise and complaining from the kids who were not selected. Xavier was thrilled and he made no attempt to hide it. It was a long walk to that house but it sure beat waiting for Kyle to slide into the seat behind him and go to work. Xavier grabbed his backpack and stood.

Mr. Bisaillon raised his hands and shouted, "Okay, that's enough! Remember what I said about homework." That quieted down most of the students. Some still grumbled their complaints at being left behind but they did so now at a much lower volume. The kids chosen to go stood and started for the front of the bus, Xavier among them.

Mr. Bisaillon stopped at the door. He turned back to his students and knelt in front of them. He lowered his voice so only his chosen companions could hear him. "Leave your backpacks here. We don't know how long we'll be walking and you don't want to carry around the extra weight."

The students obediently unslung their backpacks. They were handed over to classmates they trusted. Xavier handed his to Dawn Kitney, his sometime-partner in science class projects. She took it and wished him luck. Xavier rejoined Mr. Bisaillon's small group of rescuers by the bus door.

"Yo, Mr. Bisaillon," Kyle called from his seat.

The teacher frowned and replied, "What is it, Kyle?"

"Can't I come? I don't wanna stay here. It's boring."

Several children giggled, a few laughed aloud. Mr. Bisaillon appeared less than thrilled.

"Don't say yes, don't say yes, don't say yes," Xavier whispered as he neared his teacher. It was no secret Mr. Bisaillon – indeed most of the staff at James Buchannan – had no love for Kyle Reed. He had been a troublemaker since kindergarten and his behavior had only gotten worse in the years since. Xavier was quite certain his teacher would make the boy stay behind.

"Sure, why not?" Mr. Bisaillon said. He sounded resigned.

Xavier's heart sank into his stomach. He wanted to take back his offer to accompany his teacher. But that would be even worse. Everyone in the class would know why and they were not likely to forget over the summer. He would leave middle school and enter high school with the reputation of a coward. So he said nothing. He no longer walked excitedly to the door; his feet shuffled along the floor and his head was down. Mr. Bisaillon patted him on the back but Xavier barely noticed. He prepared himself for a long walk through the middle of nowhere with his least favorite person in the world walking beside him.

The day had started out very well. Its ending was quite the opposite.

Chapter Four

The Walk, The House, The Thing in the Woods

The good news was there was still plenty of daylight left. The sun was high and their shadows walked alongside them as the small group walked back the way they had come. Xavier looked over his shoulder and saw the bus as a small yellow object on the side of the road. The white smoke had decreased in volume and intensity when the students picked for this excursion stood beside it and Mr. Bisaillon went over the rules. By the time they started walking the white smoke had reduced itself to a thin but steady stream drifting lazily into the sky. From this distance it was no longer visible. Xavier hoped against logic that Mrs. Darby would find a way to get it started and come pick them up. His enthusiasm for finding that house diminished considerably as soon as Kyle Reed was allowed to join them.

Xavier looked at everybody but him. Mr. Bisaillon walked in the lead. Every few steps he would glance over his shoulder at his fellow walkers. The girls, Nevaeh and Maya, walked behind him. They spoke quietly amongst themselves and walked as if this were the normal outcome for a field trip. Nevaeh was the taller of the two, with skin the color of alabaster. Xavier thought she was pretty if a bit arrogant in class. She could beat him in reading, but he had it all over her in science and math.

Maya was short, with long black hair that reminded Xavier of his mom's. She could also be described as pretty. Her voice was thick with an Hispanic accent but her English was perfectly understandable. Xavier envied her a little for her bilingual ability. He often wished he could speak more than one language.

Andy was the blondest kid Xavier had ever seen. He didn't spend a lot of time around him but he knew Andy was a big Phillies fan. He often went into the city to watch his favorite team play. The only time Andy resented a Phillies loss was when it came against the Mets. On those days Andy was nearly inconsolable. Xavier was more of a basketball man himself - a huge fan of LeBron, naturally - so the two had little in common. He liked Andy enough but they rarely spoke or interacted in class, and never outside of it. In fact, Xavier realized, this was the first time the two of them were in close proximity without the benefit of being in a classroom.

Carlos walked beside Xavier. He didn't say much, which was his norm. Xavier could have used a bit of conversation and Carlos was his best bet. But the short kid with his short brown hair and short brown socks did not offer any.

Kyle was, obviously, out of the question.

That left only Mr. Bisaillon. Xavier already had enough problems with Kyle Reed. He didn't need a reputation as a teacher's pet any more than he needed that of a coward. And so Xavier walked in silence.

He checked the time on his phone. *At least that works*, he thought. It was 3:17 in the afternoon. Yes, plenty of daylight left. They just had to get to this house and talk the people there into letting them use their phone. It was likely to be quite some time before anyone could come and pick them up and bring them home. Xavier did some fast calculations and figured he wouldn't get there until well after 8, and that was if he was lucky. He was not feeling particularly lucky at the moment.

A small rock skidded past Xavier's feet. It was the third such rock he'd seen since they left the bus. As with the other two he turned and saw Kyle smiling at him. This was getting on Xavier's nerves. He doubted he could take Kyle in a fight, was almost certain he could not, but each time the other boy kicked a rock at him, Xavier felt a burning sensation behind his eyes. If they didn't find this house soon there was going to be trouble.

The group continued on, Mr. Bisaillon in the lead. They did not see a single car or truck driving in either direction. If not for the power lines just off the side of the road they could have travelled back in time 100 years. It was also quiet, *too* quiet for Xavier. He was used to the sounds of traffic and people having loud conversations up and down his street. Of sirens, either distant or near, wailing through his neighborhood. He simply wasn't used to this kind of silence.

The one upside to his current location was the smell of the air. It was cleaner out here. He had become accustomed to the smell of car exhaust and garbage, and even body odor, the latter mostly at school. Out here everything smelled different. It was pine and grass and animals and wildflowers. As unnerving as it was, he thought he could get used to it pretty easily.

The trees on the right side of the road revealed a gap in their line. What looked to be a very narrow dirt road wound its way into a dense patch of trees and foliage. The group stopped there.

"I think this is it," Mr. Bisaillon announced.

"This is what?" Andy asked.

Mr. Bisaillon pointed to the dirt road. "This is the driveway to that house. I think." The teacher stood on his toes and craned his neck. "Can't see over the trees." He regarded his students. "Maya, help me out."

"How?" the girl asked.

Mr. Bisaillon dropped to one knee. "Climb on my back, then stand up on my shoulders. I'll lift you up. See if you can spot the house."

Maya did as he asked. Her legs wobbled a bit when Mr. Bisaillon stood. "Don't worry, I won't let you fall," he assured her.

The girl looked in the direction of the dirt road. Xavier saw her squint against the sunlight. She even brought up one hand to shield her eyes and looked like a soldier saluting a giant officer. Finally she said, "I see it! Mr. Bisaillon, I see a house! It's way up at the top of a hill!"

"Good job," Mr. Bisaillon replied. He lowered the girl to the ground. "Okay, follow me." He led the way off the main road and onto the dirt driveway.

The sun vanished almost as soon as they left the pavement. The trees on either side of the driveway provided an effective canopy that threw them all into near-darkness. The warm, pleasant breeze that had followed them since they left the bus disappeared at the same time. Sounds reached their ears, coming from the woods on either side. Xavier stopped and looked each time he heard something but he could see nothing. Beyond the perimeter of trees all was darkness. A sudden chill ran down his spine. The small hairs on his arms stood up and stayed that way.

An animal that must have been much larger than the squirrels he saw in his own back yard rustled in the darkness beyond his vision. Xavier had no wish to see what it was; he looked anyway. Something moved, something big, perhaps as big as he. It raced between two large, thick trees and crouched. Xavier realized he was wrong; whatever it was it was much larger than he, larger by far even than Mr. Bisaillon. His eyes went wide. He stuttered and pointed.

"What's your problem, Valsaint? Scared of the dark?"

It was Kyle. Of course it was. He had come up behind Xavier when the smaller boy's attention had been glued to the woods. Xavier looked at him, the dread he usually felt when dealing with Kyle temporarily forgotten.

"There's something in there," Xavier said. His mouth and throat felt bone dry.

"Maybe it's your mom," Kyle replied. He shoved Xavier forward with both hands.

Xavier stumbled but managed to keep his feet under him. He never took his eyes from the woods, but whatever he saw had vanished back into the darkness.

"Keep moving, moron," Kyle said, and shoved him forward again.

Xavier started moving. Every few steps he looked into the woods again but he saw nothing. Nor did he hear anything. Whatever it was must have moved on. He didn't know why, but he felt relief at the thing's departure. As if he had narrowly escaped something hideous. He caught up to the rest of the group and they continued to follow the winding driveway.

The distinctive caw of birds reached their ears. Xavier craned his neck toward the treetops. There was not much to see but he could hear the sound of their wings. As the seven refugees from James Buchanan Middle School continued their advance up the driveway the sound became louder, more intense. "There must be a thousand birds in those trees," Xavier remarked to no one in particular.

"I don't like birds," Nevaeh announced. She cast nervous eyes at the treetops.

"Hello, Alfred Hitchcock," Mr. Bisaillon commented. When he glanced at his students and saw only blank stares he sighed. "Classical reference. Google it when we get back to civilization."

They reached a clearing in the woods and suddenly the sun was in their eyes again. The glare was intense after the darkness of the last few minutes. Xavier shielded his eyes from the sun and found himself at the bottom of a large, steep hill. At the top sat a house.

It was the largest house Xavier had ever seen. It reminded him of the photos in his history books of old English manors. He wondered if perhaps it was even larger than his school. The middle section alone looked as if it could fit every house on his street within its walls. The two end sections were nearly as large and were rounded like grain silos. He counted three levels of windows plus another, smaller set at the top of the structure. A very large deck ran the width of the front of the house and disappeared around the sides.

The grounds – this could not be called a lawn – sprawled as far as he could see. The grass was neatly manicured and flower beds dotted the border of the driveway leading to the mansion. Xavier whistled through his teeth.

"There we are," Mr. Bisaillon announced. He continued to follow the driveway up the hill. If the teacher was impressed by the spectacle he kept it to himself.

Xavier's classmates, too, marveled at the sheer size of the house. Even Kyle seemed to have forgotten about him, at least for the moment. The students stood and gazed at the mansion on the hill while their teacher made his way toward it.

After a few more moments the six children followed Mr. Bisaillon. The driveway was not notably steep however Xavier felt his legs beginning to ache. Each step he took his body weight seemed to increase. He ran a hand across his forehead and it came away wet. He wiped his hand on his pants and hoped no one noticed. The girls seemed to be having a hard time, too. They had stopped talking and giggling and were now starting to breathe heavy. A look at Andy and Carlos told him they, too, were feeling the effects of their exertion. Xavier did not bother to see if Kyle was likewise getting winded.

It seemed to take hours but the group finally crested the hill and stood at the top of the dirt driveway. The house loomed in front of them, blotting out the sun. The wind kicked up and ruffled Xavier's shirt. He closed his eyes and spread his arms and let the breeze cool his skin. It felt good, great, in fact. When he opened his eyes he saw his classmates mimicking him.

All except Kyle, of course. He simply stood with his withering gaze fixed upon Xavier. His eyes said, *Okay, I'm already over this house. Time to get back to our regularly scheduled bullying.*

"You guys stay here. I'll see if they'll let us use their phone." Mr. Bisaillon waited for his students to nod their understanding and then he mounted the steps that led to the front door. He knocked, waited. No one came to the door. He knocked again. After a few more attempts he turned back to his students. "Doesn't look like they're home."

"Maybe they're in the back," Andy offered. "I bet they couldn't hear you because they're in the back yard."

"We can give it a shot," Mr. Bisaillon replied. "You guys stay here in case someone does come to the door. Andy, come with me."

The teacher and the blonde boy walked around the side of the house.

No more than a moment after their departure, the front door creaked open.

Chapter Five

Inside the House, The Soldiers

Xavier's eyes were drawn immediately to the large double doors that were the entrance to the house. Both swung open slowly and with a loud creak. The sound alone caused Xavier's heart to beat a little faster. He, along with his classmates, waited to see who would emerge from the darkness of the house.

No one did. The doors remained open and the entryway remained empty.

"Okay, that's weird," Carlos said.

Maya turned in the direction where Mr. Bisaillon had vanished. "Mr. Bisaillon! The door's open but there ain't nobody there!"

Mr. Bisaillon did not reappear from the side of the house. Maya shouted to him again. The five students from James Buchannan Middle School remained alone.

"Don't be wussies!" Kyle exclaimed. He grabbed Xavier and Carlos by their shirts and dragged both boys up the steps. When they stood in front of the doors Kyle turned his attention to the two girls. "Get up here and stop acting like babies."

Nevaeh and Maya exchanged nervous glances.

"Yo! Anybody home?" Kyle shouted into the darkness beyond the front doors. After a moment he turned back toward the two girls. "See? Nobody there. Now get up here and let's go find a phone. I'd like to get home before the summer ends!"

The girls were clearly reluctant but they mounted the steps together. They stood behind Xavier and Carlos.

"Well? Get in there!"

Kyle shoved the two boys across the threshold. He grabbed Nevaeh's arm and prodded her forward. Maya went along. Then Kyle followed them through.

The foyer was cavernous. The vaulted ceiling was at least twenty feet above their heads. A very large light fixture – an honest-to-gosh chandelier – hung from it. Two wide staircases ascended from the foyer and met at the top of the second floor. Several hallways branched away in multiple directions. The floor was hard wood and so polished Xavier could see his reflection in its surface. Several small writing tables and a few luxurious chairs dotted the foyer.

Something about the room made Xavier uneasy. He had no idea what it could be. Nothing seemed out of place, there were no signs of obvious threat. Still the hair on his arms stood and his brow was coated with sweat.

A very large and elegant living room stood to the left of the foyer. Paintings that would not have looked out of place in the Louvre decorated the walls. End tables and coffee tables competed with large chairs and sofas. A giant stone fireplace dominated one wall. A small pile of chopped wood sat next to it. The room could have accommodated every kid in the class with enough space for the kids in Ms. Porcaro's classroom next door.

"We shouldn't be in here," Xavier whispered.

"What?" Carlos asked.

Xavier cleared his throat. "I said we shouldn't be in here. Isn't this burglary or something? We could get in trouble." That was true to the best of Xavier's knowledge but it was not the real reason he wanted to leave. It wasn't even in the top five.

Kyle barked a short, loud laugh. "You're such a wuss, Valsaint. Go find a phone, loser."

"We'll go with you," Nevaeh declared. "Me and Maya."

"Me, too," Carlos tried.

"Not even close," Kyle told him. "You're sticking with me. You three morons go that way, me and this moron will go this way."

Xavier could think of nothing else to say. Of course he wanted Carlos with him but Kyle had handed down his decree and that was that. All things considered Xavier felt fortunate; at least he had Nevaeh and Maya with him instead of looking for a phone by himself, or worse, looking with Kyle. As the group parted Xavier wondered what they would say if the owners of the house showed up. Hopefully Mr. Bisaillon would hear them coming up the driveway and explain their situation. It was a well-know, if stupid, fact of life that adults tended to listen to other adults before children. He certainly didn't relish the idea of having to explain to complete strangers what he and his classmates were doing in their home.

He walked down the hall chosen by Kyle, the two girls behind him. His companions said nothing but he could hear their shuffling footsteps and quick breathing. They were scared. Xavier couldn't blame them. *He* was scared, too. If the owners showed up now they could very easily call the cops. The last thing Xavier needed was to have to call his mom from jail. Nevertheless he decided he couldn't show his fear in front of the others. Not here, not now.

The hall was long and dark. There was muted light at the end where it opened into a room. Xavier emerged from the hall into a kitchen larger than any room in his house. The floor was white linoleum and spotless. The table was circular and surrounded by twelve wooden chairs. A narrow white door stood to the side of the stove. Xavier figured it led to a pantry; his grandmother's house had a similar door and that's where she kept most of her dry foods and cans of soup. The appliances appeared old but they, too, were very clean. Colorful plastic letter magnets adorned the fridge.   Some had been arranged into a message. OUR N W HOM , it said. "Looks like they lost all the *E*s," Maya remarked.

The phone was mounted to the wall beside the refrigerator. Xavier walked to it.

"They still have a landline," Maya commented.

"Well, duh," Nevaeh replied. "No phone signal out here, remember?"

"Oh, right."

Xavier removed the handset from the cradle and placed it against his ear. He heard no dial tone. He hung up and tried again. "It doesn't work," he told the girls.

"Great," Nevaeh said. "Now what?"

As Xavier hung up the phone he caught movement out of the corner of his eye. He turned in the direction of an open doorway that led from the kitchen into another part of the house. Something had moved from the doorway, something that might have been there the whole time. Xavier gasped. The girls turned quickly toward the doorway.

"What? What is it?" Maya asked.

"There...There was someone standing there."

"Who?" This time it was Nevaeh's turn to ask.

Xavier craned his neck but he could not see into the hallway beyond the door. His first thought was to walk over and see if whoever-it-was was still there. But his legs refused to work. He stood by the phone as if his feet had grown roots into the floor.

Nevaeh's eyes took on a defiant glare. "Don't try to scare us, Xavier," she declared. The girl walked to the doorway and looked beyond. She stood there for a moment before turning her eyes to Xavier. "There's no one there. No. One. You're a jerk for trying to scare us. I'm gonna tell Mr. Bisaillon."

Xavier felt his ability to move return. He approached the doorway slowly, still craning his neck. Nevaeh was correct; the hall beyond was empty. It stretched quite a way and he counted no fewer than six doors along the walls. "I know I saw something. I thought it was a kid but I didn't get a good enough look."

"Whatever," Nevaeh announced. "Let's go find Mr. Bisaillon." She marched back the way they had come, Maya walking in step behind her.

Xavier remained in the kitchen. His eyes travelled to the large bay window that took up most of one wall. Maybe whoever he saw had gone outside. Xavier approached the window. Beyond the glass stretched the back yard of the property. Like the front the lawn was neatly mowed, the various flower gardens and trees trimmed. It sloped down toward what Xavier assumed to be more woods.

Mr. Bisaillon and Andy were back there. He saw his teacher fiddling with his cell phone. After a few moments he shook his head at Andy. The blonde boy appeared irritated. Xavier could not hear their conversation but he could guess what was going on.

Something beyond the two in the back yard caught Xavier's attention. Something moved near the downward slope of the well-manicured grounds. Xavier squinted against the glare thrown by the window glass. Someone was walking up the hill in the direction of the house. *Finally*, Xavier thought. *The owner must have been down the hill and we didn't see him*.

He was about to follow the girls back to the foyer when he saw the man walking up the hill was not alone. A second man appeared, then a third. In a few seconds there were dozens of them. Nor were they walking. Xavier searched for the right word. After a moment it came to him. These men were *marching*. They moved in lockstep with one another like the clone troopers in the *Star Wars* movies. To reinforce the image these men wore uniforms. Some were blue, others, gray, but they were pretty close in design. Each man carried what appeared to be a rifle, the long stock held against their shoulder.

Mr. Bisaillon and Andy turned and saw the soldiers marching in their direction. Andy retreated a few steps. Mr. Bisaillon seemed uncertain of what to do. He shouted something at them but the soldiers seemed not to reply. They never broke stride.

Andy grabbed at his teacher's arm and tried to pull him back. Mr. Bisaillon seemed unable to take his eyes from these new arrivals.

The soldiers swung their rifles up and pointed them in the direction of the pair in front of them. Xavier gasped.

Mr. Bisaillon grabbed Andy's hand and bolted for the front of the house.

Xavier ran, too. He reached the foyer to find the girls standing by the front door.

Maya was fighting to maintain control but it seemed obvious she was scared and trying not to cry. Nevaeh's voice held a measure of alarm when she announced, "The door's locked! It won't open!"

Carlos and Kyle appeared atop the landing where the twin staircases met and looked down at them. "What's the matter?" Carlos asked. The expression on the faces of the girls seemed to unnerve him. He sounded scared, too.

"We're locked in!" Nevaeh told him.

"Let me try," Xavier offered. Nevaeh got out of his way.

Before Xavier could try his luck Kyle descended the stairs and shouldered his way to the door. "Back up, all of ya," he ordered. The other kids did as they were told. Kyle pulled on the door handle. It made an unpleasant squeak but it did not open. Kyle stood back, regarded the door.

"We can't be trapped in here!" Maya exclaimed.

"Shut up," Kyle told her.

He tried again. The squeak repeated itself, more loudly this time. Xavier saw the door quiver in its frame.

Kyle must have seen it, too. He pulled with what looked to be all his strength. The door flew open. Kyle, off-balance, flew back and crashed into one of the small writing tables. He grunted with pain.

Nevaeh and Maya were through the door in an instant, but both girls stopped in their tracks after making it only a few steps onto the deck. They screamed in unison. Xavier raced out after them.

The soldiers he had seen out back had moved to the front of the house. They marched in formation toward the front deck.

"Get inside! Get inside!"

The shout had come from the side of the house, very close. Xavier saw Mr. Bisaillon and Andy running at full speed for the front deck. Behind them came the soldiers he had seen from the kitchen window. *Now there are* two *groups*, Xavier thought, panicked.

He grabbed Nevaeh and Maya and shoved them through the front door. Xavier lost his balance and fell. The hard wood of the deck bruised his knee and made him gasp. Still he was on his feet a second later and limping for the front door. He threw himself inside the house and turned his head in the direction of the door.

Mr. Bisaillon and Andy neared the steps. Some of the soldiers in the front yard beat them to it. Xavier watched his teacher and his classmate disappear into a wall of blue and gray uniforms. He lost sight of them, although from the actions and body language of the soldiers it seemed a fight was happening. The mass of blue and gray seemed to push itself farther from the front deck, carrying both teacher and student with it.

It was instinct, not conscious thought, that moved Xavier in their direction. They needed help. He did not get far.

The trees that bordered the property exploded in an enormous black cloud. Its shape was inconsistent, with patches of daylight shining through some areas and nothing but black in others. It took Xavier a full five seconds to realize what he was looking at. Birds. Thousands of them, maybe tens of thousands. They were flying directly at the house.

The front door slammed itself closed with so much force the wood frame cracked. Xavier reeled back, his feet unable to stop his backward tumble. He landed on Kyle, who swore but seemed incapable of freeing himself from the sudden weight lying atop him.

Xavier rolled free of the other boy. That was going to cost him for sure. Kyle wouldn't care if Xavier meant to flatten him or not. He had done the deed, and he did it in front of everyone. Kyle's revenge would not be pleasant.

Xavier started to rise. A wave of nausea washed over him and dropped him to his knees again. He felt the bile rise in his throat but somehow he stopped himself from vomiting. The world seemed to shimmer around him as if he were in the middle of a heat mirage. Everything blurred and rippled and Xavier closed his eyes tight against the visual assault. The floor trembled beneath him. The hardwood felt strange and unusual. His stomach dropped into his feet; the sensation reminded him of riding the rollercoaster at the summer carnival in Wilkes-Barre. He might have whimpered and he might have produced no sound at all. His senses overwhelmed, he could do nothing but wait for the world to return to normal.

A few moments later it did. When it passed he wiped his eyes and looked again at the front door.

It had changed. In point of fact, the entire foyer had changed. The hardwood floor, so shiny he had seen his own reflection in its surface, was old and faded and pitted with cracks and small holes. The double front doors had likewise lost their luster. They were in the same shape as the floor.

Xavier's gaze moved about the foyer. The ornate staircases looked in danger of collapse. The railings were gone, the steps rotted. The chandelier lay in the middle of the foyer like a dead monster, its elegant crystal shattered into thousands of pieces. The writing tables had disintegrated into heaps of brittle, aged wood.

The living room had fared no better. The paintings were faded and some hung at odd angles. The tables and furniture had collapsed into unrecognizable heaps of rotting garbage. Some of the stones from the fireplace had fallen out and lay on the floor. The chopped wood that would have fueled the fireplace on a cold Pennsylvania night had long since decayed into pulp.

His classmates gazed in horror at the state of the foyer. Whatever hit Xavier had hit them, as well. Carlos and the girls were rising to their knees. Kyle still lay curled into a ball near the remains of one of the writing tables. His body shook and it sounded to Xavier as if the bigger boy might be crying.

Carlos, his voice a hoarse croak, was the only one who spoke. "Oh, boy."

Chapter Six

Surrounded

Xavier's knee barked at him when he tried to stand. He grimaced and rubbed the sore spot. He watched Carlos regain his feet and help the girls stand. Nevaeh recovered quickly from whatever produced that wave of nausea and she moved toward the front doors. For an awful moment Xavier thought she might actually open them. The girl instead peeked through the now-cracked glass that bordered the doors. She gasped.

"Mr. Bisaillon and Andy!" she shouted.

Xavier finally got to his feet and limped to her. He looked through the glass.

The soldiers stood in an organized line, their weapons resting against their shoulders. Mr. Bisaillon was on his hands and knees, clearly struggling to rise. His tie was gone and his shirt torn. Blood seeped slowly from his nose. Andy, looking in better shape than his teacher and kneeling next to him, helped Mr. Bisaillon to his knees. Both placed their hands behind their head after one of the soldiers barked something at them.

So focused was he on what was happening to his teacher and classmate, it took Xavier a few moments to note the changes that had taken place outside the house.

The deck was rotted and worn. Several boards were missing and large holes dotted its once-pristine appearance. The front yard had also changed. The grass was no longer neatly cut. In fact, it looked as if it had not seen a lawn mower since before Xavier was born. The grass was tall and full of weeds. The soldiers stood in formation, their rifles resting on their shoulders. A few of them, most likely officers, paced back and forth among the lines, barking orders Xavier could not hear. Four of them stood guard next to Andy and Mr. Bisaillon.

"They're gonna kill em!" Nevaeh exclaimed.

"Please, no!" Maya screamed. She began to cry.

The soldiers made no move to harm their teacher or their classmate. They stood in their formation and neither moved nor spoke.

"Hang on," Xavier told them. "They're not doing anything, just standing there."

Carlos and Maya joined them. The four kids jostled one another for a look outside.

"They're gonna come in here," Carlos said to no one in particular.

"What do we do then? Maya asked.

"We can't possibly stop them." Xavier did not realize he had spoken aloud until he noticed the other kids staring at him in varying degrees of fear. He shrugged. What else could he say?

"We can get out the back," Carlos suggested. "If all these guys are out front there's no one in the back yard." He started back toward the kitchen. The girls followed.

"Hang on," Xavier told them. When they paused he continued, "Are we not gonna talk about what just happened? Look at this house."

His three classmates did indeed look, but only a momentary, cursory glance. None seemed to want to take it all in. Or perhaps they were incapable of doing so. Xavier was as reluctant as they but this seemed to be their reality now.

"I'm heading for the back," Carlos informed him. "You coming?"

The girls nodded their agreement and the three of them disappeared quickly down the hallway which led to the kitchen.

Xavier was about to join them when he saw Kyle getting to his feet.

"You okay?"

Kyle wiped his nose and sniffled. For a half-second he was no longer the bully. He looked small and scared and vulnerable. Then his eyes hardened and his hands balled into fists. "Shut up, idiot."

Xavier shook his head. *Well, that didn't last long.* With a final look around the foyer and the living room he headed for the kitchen. He heard Kyle fall into step behind him.

The change that had overtaken the whole front of the house had also transformed the kitchen. The linoleum was cracked and worn. The refrigerator lay on the floor much like the chandelier in the foyer. The letter magnets were scattered about and covered with dust. The cabinet doors, the ones that remained, hung from rusted hinges. The shelves inside were barren. The old phone was gone; its cord lay on the floor like a dead snake. The large table still stood in the middle of the room but it swayed a bit when Xavier bumped it on his way past.

The door Xavier assumed lead to the pantry was still in place. Its paint had faded somewhat but it seemed mostly unaffected by what had happened.

Carlos, Nevaeh and Maya stood by the windows. Their body language told Xavier what he would see even before he joined them.

There were more soldiers standing in the tall grass of the back yard. They stood and stared at the four young people at the windows.

Carlos swallowed loudly. "There's a lot more of those guys than I thought."

"So we're surrounded?" Maya's voice was high-pitched. She was close to panic, if she wasn't there already.

Xavier's eyes were drawn to the blue sky above. The birds moved in tight formation, forming a black circle that orbited above the house and the grounds. Even from inside the ruined kitchen he could hear their caws and squawks. He turned away from the door.

Xavier pulled out his cell phone again. Before he hit the power button he prayed for a few bars, or even one. One might be enough. He exhaled loudly when he saw the same NO SERVICE message that had greeted him since the school bus broke down.

Nevaeh looked at the phone. "Wait a minute," she said. "Upstairs! We might be able to get a signal upstairs!"

"Damn, you're a moron." Kyle stood behind them. His eyes moved from the window to Nevaeh.

"Think about it," Nevaeh continued, ignoring Kyle completely. "This place is huge. The top floor is really high up. It might work."

"It's worth a shot," Xavier agreed.

Kyle shook his head. "The basement's a better idea."

Nevaeh placed her hands on her hips. "By what stretch of the imagination is the basement a better idea? You think we'll get reception down there? Now who's the moron?"

Kyle's eyes flared. He took an angry step toward Nevaeh. Xavier thought he might actually hit the girl. And he may have, had Carlos not gotten between them. It took Xavier only a moment to join the other boy. Kyle stopped in his tracks. His whole body quivered. Xavier thought at first Kyle was angry enough to take all three of them, four if Maya came to her friend's defense. But it was not anger he saw in the bigger boy's eyes. And the quivering was not of rage. Kyle was scared. That simple realization chilled Xavier. Kyle was the toughest kid in the entire school. If *he* was this scared...

"Let's just hear him out," Xavier offered. He looked closely at Kyle. He still didn't know if the bigger boy would swing on them or not. Xavier braced himself and said, "What about the basement?"

Kyle continued to glare at his classmates but Xavier's offer seemed to placate him, if only marginally. After another moment he licked his lips and said, "This old place was probably built a hundred years ago, maybe two hundred. There might be a tunnel in the basement."

Carlos sighed and rolled his eyes.

"Where'd you get that idea?" Maya asked. She now stood next to Nevaeh.

"In history class, idiot! Remember when Miss DiBella told us about the Underground Railroad? She said some houses had escape tunnels for slaves." His eyes moved rapidly across the faces of his classmates as if he were searching for the least sign of agreement. "Don't you get it? This could be one of those!"

"That's pretty thin," Carlos admitted.

"Like Valsaint said, it's worth a shot!" Kyle exclaimed. Some of the fear had left his voice. It was replaced by the usual anger and contempt Kyle Reed usually showed everyone around him.

Nevaeh sidestepped Carlos and Xavier and stood in front of Kyle. "Then you go down there and the rest of us will go upstairs and see if we can get a signal."

"Hold up," Xavier told them. He agreed with Carlos. What Kyle was suggesting was ridiculous. He did not for one moment think there was a tunnel in the basement, assuming the house even had a basement. But if Kyle turned out to be correct Xavier had no doubt the boy would follow that tunnel and leave the rest of them behind. The thought of Kyle Reed emerging into the sunlight a few miles beyond the house and those soldiers while Xavier and the others were still trapped inside...

"Okay, Kyle, go find the basement. Carlos, go with him. I'll try upstairs with Maya and Nevaeh."

Kyle seemed at least somewhat placated. He licked his lips again and nodded.

"I'm not going down into the basement," Carlos argued.

"Scared, Medina? I always knew you were a wuss," Kyle sneered. He seemed to have regained much of his usual bravado.

"Hey, I ain't no wuss," Carlos exclaimed. He was angry, that much was clear. He took a step toward Kyle.

"Oh, come on! Are we really gonna fight now? With all those guys outside? Shouldn't we be trying to get out of here and get some help for Mr. Bisaillon and Andy?"

"Xavier's right," Maya said. She looked out the window again before turning back to the others. "I don't think those guys are gonna wait all day. Sooner or later they're gonna come in here. We need to get out before then."

"Why does it have to be me?" Carlos asked.

"Fine, I'll go," Nevaeh told them. "I don't care. But Maya's right. We need to get a move on."

"You two look for the basement, the rest of us will head upstairs." Xavier spoke in his calmest tone of voice. "Deal?"

"Fine," Kyle agreed. "Meet back in the foyer in about ten minutes. Let's go, Nevaeh."

Nevaeh hugged Maya and followed Kyle out of the kitchen. Maya watched her friend leave.

"Let's head up," Xavier said. "The sooner we get out of here the better."

The three friends headed in the direction of the foyer.

Chapter Seven

The Basement, The Man-Thing and The Woman

There were several doors along each side of the hall. The first led into a study. Ancient bookshelves held equally ancient books. They looked as if they would crumble to dust if Kyle so much as got close to them. The second opened into a playroom of some kind. Old toys made of wood and metal and some very decrepit armchairs filled the room. Kyle could picture long-dead adults sitting in those chairs watching equally-long-dead children playing with those toys. He shrugged. Whatever. The third door led to a bathroom. Kyle did not even step inside, although he toyed with the idea of shoving Nevaeh in there and holding the door closed. While the thought of that made him smile he knew the girl would scream her head off and he simply didn't want to hear it.

"Did anyone try that door in the kitchen?" Nevaeh asked.

Kyle stopped. Had they? No, he was pretty sure they had not. He felt stupid—not for the first time—and he doubled back for the kitchen. He just knew Nevaeh was behind him trying not to laugh at his obvious stupidity. Kyle resisted the urge to turn on the girl and swing with everything he had.

When they reached the narrow door in the kitchen Kyle tried the handle. It turned easily enough and he swung the door open. A wood staircase led down into absolute darkness. Kyle felt along either side of the door. He found the light switch and flicked it several times but the bulb was out. Or missing.

"Great," Kyle said. "Get out your phone so we can see where we're going."

Nevaeh did as he said. She held her phone out in front of her. Its meager light illuminated a few of the steps that had been cloaked in darkness but nothing beyond.

"Head down."

Nevaeh turned to Kyle. "*You* head down. I'm not going first."

"You have the phone, genius."

Nevaeh shoved her phone at Kyle.

He sneered and took it. "Even Medina would have been better," he shot as he edged past her. The step creaked under his weight but not loudly. He took another tentative step, Nevaeh's phone held out in front of him like a shield. "Let's go."

Nevaeh waited until Kyle had descended several steps before she followed him. The steps seemed solid enough. He felt the girl place one hand on his shoulder.

The last step creaked very loudly. The sound was like a rifle shot in the darkness. Nevaeh gasped but stopped herself short of a full scale scream. Her fingernails drove into Kyle's shoulders and he hissed and turned on her.

"Sorry," she offered.

Kyle muttered "Watch it!" under his breath.

He waved her phone in a slow arc in front of him. The basement was full of large, dark shapes. The light from the girls' phone was simply not bright enough to make out anything.

"Can you see anything? Because I can't."

"Not much," Kyle admitted. "Lots of stuff down here. Can't really tell what it is. Let's try this way."

They advanced slowly into the basement. The floor felt like dirt beneath Kyle's sneakers. Although he could not see much of anything he got the impression the room was enormous, maybe the size of the gym back at school. And it smelled. He could not identify what it smelled like but it was not a pleasant odor. Mildew, maybe, or simply age. Kyle wondered how long it had been since anyone had been down here.

"Is it me or is it really cold down here?"

"Would you shut up?" Kyle hissed. But she was right. He had already repressed one shiver and he could feel more on the way. The basement was cold and getting colder the farther in they ventured.

Large shapes loomed at the edges of the phone's light. Furniture, probably. They glimpsed something covered with a sheet. An old dresser, perhaps. His grandmother had very old and very large dressers in her house. What had she called them? It was a funny-sounding name but he could not remember at the moment.

"I don't like it down here," Nevaeh announced. "It smells bad."

"So does your mom. Now be quiet."

He half-expected her to get mad and stomp back up the stairs, probably throwing a few choice words in his direction as she went. But she remained behind him, her hands on his shoulders, and said nothing.

They came upon an ancient piano. Kyle tapped a few of the keys. The notes sounded sickly and died in the stale air. He took some pleasure when Nevaeh jumped at the sounds.

"Kyle, please, let's just see if there's a tunnel so we can get out of here."

There was fear in her voice. On a normal day he would find that to be very satisfying. Then again, on a normal day, they wouldn't be in the basement of an old house that looked new when they first saw it, and their teacher wouldn't be outside surrounded by creepy-looking idiots dressed in old Army uniforms. And anyway, Nevaeh was right. They did need to find a way out. He moved away from the piano.

Kyle noticed for the first time his breath was frosting the air. He could see it in the light from Nevaeh's phone.

This is definitely not right. Why is it so damned cold down here? He pushed the question away. He didn't care. What he did care about was finding a way out of this dump.

There were more large objects in front of them. Kyle moved past these slowly, shining the phone's light in front of him. In a few moments they reached the foundation wall. Several old and broken chairs were piled in a heap between them and the wall. He moved the light this way and that but he succeeded only in throwing shadows around. He could not tell if there was anything on the other side of the chairs other than a rock wall. No tunnel there.

"Okay, let's try over there." He started to move to his right, Nevaeh still behind him, still digging her fingernails into his shoulders.

Something growled in the darkness.

Nevaeh shrieked. Kyle winced at the pain in his ears. The girl bolted away. Kyle backed up. The phone's light revealed nothing in front of him but he had heard the growl, plain as day. He jumped a little when he heard Nevaeh all but fly up the stairs. He turned and headed in that direction.

He found the staircase easily enough. The bottom step creaked loudly again under his weight. At the top he could see the cellar door slowly swinging closed. Kyle bolted up the stairs.

One of them gave way under his feet. For a split-second he was sure the entire thing would collapse and he would be back down in the basement, alone with whatever it was that growled at them. His hands, however, had other ideas. They grasped the old railing and kept him from falling. It took a few seconds but he managed to free his foot from the splintered wood of the broken step.

At the top he could see only a sliver of light where the door was about to close. He moved as fast as he could. The door closed just as he reached it. He fumbled for the knob and turned it. The door did not budge. He pushed again. Nothing. Had Nevaeh locked him inside? If that was the case she would soon be exploring entirely new realms of pain when he got out. Girl or not, no one was going to get away with locking him down here.

The bottom step creaked.

Kyle's heart nearly stopped. His hands went numb and he dropped Nevaeh's phone. It bounced on one of the steps and then fell through. It must have broken when it hit the floor because its light vanished and plunged Kyle into complete darkness.

Whatever had reached the bottom step was coming his way. He could hear it getting closer, could hear the other steps groan beneath its weight.

Kyle turned and threw all his weight against the door. It rattled in its frame but did not open. He felt dust drifting down around him. He beat his numb fists against the door. "Let me out! Let me out! Help!"

He felt something warm on the back of his neck. It was the thing's breath. Kyle froze. All thoughts of retribution against Nevaeh flew from his mind. He likewise forgot all about his classmates searching the upper floors and about Mr. Bisaillon and Andy. In fact, he forgot about everything.

His legs felt as if they were made of rubber. He swayed and nearly fell over. Something big and strong caught him and kept him from tumbling down the stairs. Something that felt like an animal's paw, impossibly large and coarse, grabbed the back of his shirt collar and dragged him down into the darkness of the basement. Kyle did not resist; his body was on automatic pilot.

The large and powerful thing took him down the steps and around to where it had growled at him. It applied pressure to Kyle's shoulder and the boy knelt in the hard, cold dirt.

Kyle blinked. Almost without realizing he had moved he wiped at the cold sweat on his forehead. As his mind started to focus again he felt himself gulping air. He tried to swallow but his throat was dry. He shivered, felt a cold breeze on his arms and on his face and neck. The thing that had brought him back down to the basement walked in front of him and stood perhaps five feet away. Kyle's eyes must have adjusted to the near-complete darkness because he could see the thing's shape, a shadow among shadows. It was big, *very* big, but it looked to be a man. Except its right hand. It was shaggy and ended in sharp claws.

"Do not be frightened."

It was not the man-thing which spoke. This was a woman's voice. It was sweet, soothing.

Kyle's breathing continued to accelerate. His head swam. He felt as if he might pass out.

Another shadow separated itself from the darkness and stood next to the man-thing. It was clearly a woman but he could see no detail beyond her silhouette.

"Such a scared little boy," she whispered. "But why? We have done nothing to hurt you." She may have placed her hand on the man-thing's arm; it was difficult to tell in the darkness. "We don't want to hurt you. Isn't that right?"

Her companion grunted.

She stepped closer until she stood directly in front of Kyle. Her voice was the delicate purr of a kitten. "In fact, we would like to help you." She knelt in front of Kyle. One of her fingers pressed gently beneath his chin and forced him to look at her.

Kyle recoiled at once. The woman's fingers were cold, so cold his muscles began to shiver. He no longer cared about escaping the basement or finding a way out of the house or even of making it back home to his mother. His list of wishes had dwindled to just one. He never wanted to be touched by this woman again, as long as he lived.

Fearing she might grasp him more forcefully if he did not look at her, he turned his head back in her direction and opened his eyes to just a slit. Kyle still could not make out much in the way of detail but something about the woman made him think of a bird. His eyes focused on hers. They were bright red and devoid of pupils. The woman's lips pulled back from her teeth. It might have been a smile but Kyle was focused on the sharp fangs that revealed themselves.

"We would certainly like to help you, Kyle. Oh, yes, we would. But first, you have to do something for us. What do you say? Do we have a deal?"

Her hands came to rest gently on Kyle's shoulders. They were cold, as if the woman had just come inside after escaping a raging blizzard. Ice crystals formed on his shirt beneath her hands.

Kyle stuttered. From somewhere very far away he heard himself say, "Yes."

"Wonderful," the woman purred. "Let us talk."

Chapter Eight

Three Different Directions, Shawn's Room

As Kyle and Nevaeh were beginning their descent into the basement, Xavier looked through the cracked windows on either side of the front door. The soldiers were still there, standing amid the high grass. He could just make out the top of Andy's head, the boy's hands still clasped behind it. He could not see Mr. Bisaillon, but every few seconds Andy would cast a worried glance beside him. The boy's expression told Xavier their teacher was still there, likely still unconscious. The black birds wheeled through the sky, squawking and cawing. Their pace seemed to have slowed somewhat but their orbit of the property continued uninterrupted.

"What's happening out there?" Maya asked.

"Same thing that was happening before," Xavier replied.

He turned from the windows and regarded the dilapidated staircase. Under any other circumstance Xavier would never trust it. It looked as if it would collapse if someone so much as sneezed near it. But these circumstances were anything but ordinary. Xavier approached it and placed one foot on the bottom step. It creaked but held his weight. He took the second step, ready to spring backward if he felt it giving way. It seemed solid enough. He turned to his classmates.

"We go one at a time. Maya, you follow me, Carlos you go third."

They nodded their agreement. Carlos grumbled at his placement but otherwise there were no objections.

It was slow going up their stairs but after several moments the three students from Mr. Bisaillon's eighth grade class stood on the second floor landing. Two narrow passages led to the right and to the left and a wide hallway lay before them, heading toward the back of the house, if Xavier was any judge of direction.

"Now what?" Maya asked.

"Three different directions, three of us," Xavier replied.

"Okay, I *know* you're not suggesting we should split up. Have you ever even *seen* a scary movie?"

"She has a point," Carlos added.

Xavier frowned. Carlos had tried to sound nonchalant but it was clear he was frightened. Not that Xavier could blame him.

"If you two want to stick together, fine. Pick a direction. Check your cells every minute or so. If you get a signal, shout. I'll do the same."

"Okay," Carlos agreed. "We'll go down there." He indicated the left hallway with a nod of his head.

"Meet back here in ten minutes. Good luck."

Xavier watched them go but only for a moment. He eyed the wide hallway that led toward the back of the house. A large window at the end of the hallway allowed some light through its dust-covered and cracked glass. The hallway on the right sported several doors along the walls but was much darker.

One of those doors might lead to an attic, he thought. *The higher up, the better, if you want to get a signal.* Xavier took the hallway to the right.

The light from that large window all but vanished after he took a few steps. Xavier pulled out his cell and turned it on. His wallpaper image (the Avengers battling Thanos) was bright enough but still managed to provide only limited light. He tried the first door and the knob turned easily in his hand. Xavier pushed the door open.

It looked as if the room might have belonged to a little girl. A small bed, its frame collapsed and its sheets decayed, lay near the far wall. The closet, its doors rotted and hanging by the top hinges, revealed ancient dresses and skirts. Some toys lay scattered about. Xavier checked his cell, tried not to be surprised that he still had no signal.

The door across from the girl's room opened into a bathroom. It was in much the same shape as the rest of the house.

Xavier had to step over a rather large hole in the floor before he made it to the next set of doors. The first was locked. Dust drifted down lazily when he tried the knob.

He regarded it and thought he was strong enough to force it open. On the other hand, the door across from it was slightly ajar. He decided on that one, first.

It was once a playroom, that much was obvious. More toys lay scattered about the floor, all covered with dust. Two small bookshelves stood next to each other against the wall to his right. Their shelves had collapsed, dumping their contents onto the floor.

Xavier knelt in the dust and picked up one of the books. The cover was devoid of any picture but the title was *The Pickwick Papers* by Charles Dickens. "The *Christmas Carol* guy?" Xavier turned the book over in his hand and a large chunk of the middle pages full out. Dust plumed up when the pages landed on the floor. Xavier grimaced and waved his hand in front of his face. He had already had enough of this room.

He checked the batter power on his phone once he was again in the hallway. He still had a charge of 82%. "That would be great if I could get a dammed signal," he said to no one.

He reached the next set of doors and paused. Something farther down the hallway caught his eye. He approached another doorway and shined his phone's meager light on it. The door that was once there was gone. At first Xavier thought it must have rotted and fallen inside the room. In fact, pieces of it lay on the floor just across the threshold, but it did not appear as if the door had rotted away. Something about the pattern of the debris suggested something else.

Something smashed this door down. Something big and strong. Xavier gulped. Before he could stop himself he began imagining the strength required to do such a thing. The hairs on his arms stood up straight again, as if mimicking the soldiers standing at attention outside. *Just find a signal and get out of here*, a voice shouted in his head. *That's enough sightseeing.*

"Got that right," Xavier replied to the voice.

For some reason the air smelled better near the doorway. He stepped inside the room.

It was a boy's bedroom. The years since its last occupant had slept in here could not disguise the fact. Despite its ancient appearance Xavier was reminded of his own room at home. Even the layout was similar, although his room was maybe one-quarter the size. One of the windows was open; a light, steady breeze wafted inside and stirred little dust devils to dance on the pitted hardwood. The boy's bed lay on the floor in front of the window. Xavier approached it.

The air was indeed fresher near the window. Xavier stood in front of it and breathed deeply. He had not realized until that moment the smell of decay and age that had overtaken the house since its…what? Change? No, that wasn't the right word. It wasn't big enough to describe what had happened just as the soldiers showed up outside. After a moment, it came to him. It's *transformation*. His English teacher, Mrs. Gauvin, would be proud of him. *Assuming you see her again*, the voice in his head chimed in. "Shut up," Xavier told it. He was starting to dislike that voice.

He peeked outside. The window looked out on the front yard. From this height he could see the assembled soldiers quite clearly. He could also see Andy and Mr. Bisaillon. The teacher had recovered and now knelt in the tall grass with his hands behind his head, the mirror image of Andy.

He cast a nervous eye at the black birds. They seemed much closer than they had from downstairs. He was able to pick out individual birds in the black mass that maintained that tight circle of darkness in the bright blue sky.

Xavier turned his eyes back to Mr. Bisaillon. He wanted to shout something, anything, to get his teacher's attention. He very nearly did. He stopped himself when it occurred to him he would also draw the attention of the soldiers. The thought of them swinging their rifles toward his window and opening fire killed any thought of trying to shout to Mr. Bisaillon.

Xavier looked at his phone. His lips pursed. He could not do anything to draw the soldiers' attention, but perhaps he was up high enough they would not notice movement in the window. Slowly, expecting the air to erupt in gunfire, Xavier held his phone outside the window. He peeked with one eye at the upper left corner of the screen.

His heart nearly leaped from his chest. The usual message of NO SERVICE was gone, replaced by a single bar. "Oh my God, oh my God," he whispered. Quickly he brought the phone inside and hit the *Recent* icon. The display obediently changed to a list of all the recent numbers he had texted and called. He selected the one labeled MOM and hit it. Nothing happened. No ringing, no elapsed time ticking by. He regarded the phone again. The familiar NO SERVICE message had returned.

Frustrated but not deterred, Xavier again held the phone outside the window.

A high-pitched scream cut through the air. Xavier yelped and jumped back from the window. He felt the phone fly from his fingers and then he was flat on his back. "No!" He scrambled to his feet and all but leaped for the window. He reached it just in time to see his phone disappear into the tall grass below. "No no no *no!*" he shouted.

For an awful moment Xavier pictured himself leaping from the window, following the path of his phone. He could not have lost it, not when he had finally managed to get a signal. He may even have done just that, if not for the soldiers looking up at him and swinging their rifles in his direction.

Xavier cast one long, heartbroken look at the spot where his phone had vanished before he threw himself onto the bed. He curled into a tight ball with his arms covering his head, waiting for the volley of fire to shred the wall next to him.

He did hear several shouts from outside, but the soldiers held their fire. It took several moments for Xavier to realize they were not going to launch a barrage of gunfire in his direction. Slowly, tentatively, he opened up. He dared not look outside again, despite the sudden and continuous clamor that reached his ears. On hands and knees he crawled from the bed. He cast a final look over his shoulder at the window and his lost phone. As he did he bumped into something.

Xavier looked forward. A pair of boots stood directly in front of him. Every muscle in his body froze instantly. *Those boots weren't there a minute ago*, the voice in his head informed him. *No kidding*, Xavier thought back. His eyes moved on their own. They followed the boots up to a pair of blue leggings. Then a black leather belt. On the side of the belt was a long sheath. What could only be a sword handle protruded from that sheath. Xavier's eyes continued their slow climb.

Above the belt was a blue shirt with silver buttons down the center. Two gloved hands hung on either side of the shirt. A single stripe (*a chevron*, the voice informed him, *remember? From Miss DiBella's second marking period history class?*) adorned each sleeve near the shoulder. Atop it all was the face of the man inside the uniform.

Man? A kid, maybe only a year or two older than Xavier. The kid-soldier looked down upon him, his face expressionless.

The world suddenly swam out of focus. Xavier felt his arms buckle and then his cheek rested upon the cold hardwood of a little boy's bedroom. He remembered nothing after that.

Chapter Nine

Three Different Directions, Shawn's Room

As Kyle and Nevaeh were beginning their descent into the basement, Xavier looked through the cracked windows on either side of the front door. The soldiers were still there, standing amid the high grass. He could just make out the top of Andy's head, the boy's hands still clasped behind it. He could not see Mr. Bisaillon, but every few seconds Andy would cast a worried glance beside him. The boy's expression told Xavier their teacher was still there, likely still unconscious. The black birds wheeled through the sky, squawking and cawing. Their pace seemed to have slowed somewhat but their orbit of the property continued uninterrupted.

"What's happening out there?" Maya asked.

"Same thing that was happening before," Xavier replied.

He turned from the windows and regarded the dilapidated staircase. Under any other circumstance Xavier would never trust it. It looked as if it would collapse if someone so much as sneezed near it. But these circumstances were anything but ordinary. Xavier approached it and placed one foot on the bottom step. It creaked but held his weight. He took the second step, ready to spring backward if he felt it giving way. It seemed solid enough. He turned to his classmates.

"We go one at a time. Maya, you follow me, Carlos you go third."

They nodded their agreement. Carlos grumbled at his placement but otherwise there were no objections.

It was slow going up their stairs but after several moments the three students from Mr. Bisaillon's eighth grade class stood on the second floor landing. Two narrow passages led to the right and to the left and a wide hallway lay before them, heading toward the back of the house, if Xavier was any judge of direction.

"Now what?" Maya asked.

"Three different directions, three of us," Xavier replied.

"Okay, I *know* you're not suggesting we should split up. Have you ever even *seen* a scary movie?"

"She has a point," Carlos added.

Xavier frowned. Carlos had tried to sound nonchalant but it was clear he was frightened. Not that Xavier could blame him.

"If you two want to stick together, fine. Pick a direction. Check your cells every minute or so. If you get a signal, shout. I'll do the same."

"Okay," Carlos agreed. "We'll go down there." He indicated the left hallway with a nod of his head.

"Meet back here in ten minutes. Good luck."

Xavier watched them go but only for a moment. He eyed the wide hallway that led toward the back of the house. A large window at the end of the hallway allowed some light through its dust-covered and cracked glass. The hallway on the right sported several doors along the walls but was much darker.

One of those doors might lead to an attic, he thought. *The higher up, the better, if you want to get a signal.* Xavier took the hallway to the right.

The light from that large window all but vanished after he took a few steps. Xavier pulled out his cell and turned it on. His wallpaper image (the Avengers battling Thanos) was bright enough but still managed to provide only limited light. He tried the first door and the knob turned easily in his hand. Xavier pushed the door open.

It looked as if the room might have belonged to a little girl. A small bed, its frame collapsed and its sheets decayed, lay near the far wall. The closet, its doors rotted and hanging by the top hinges, revealed ancient dresses and skirts. Some toys lay scattered about. Xavier checked his cell, tried not to be surprised that he still had no signal.

The door across from the girl's room opened into a bathroom. It was in much the same shape as the rest of the house.

Xavier had to step over a rather large hole in the floor before he made it to the next set of doors. The first was locked. Dust drifted down lazily when he tried the knob.

He regarded it and thought he was strong enough to force it open. On the other hand, the door across from it was slightly ajar. He decided on that one, first.

It was once a playroom, that much was obvious. More toys lay scattered about the floor, all covered with dust. Two small bookshelves stood next to each other against the wall to his right. Their shelves had collapsed, dumping their contents onto the floor.

Xavier knelt in the dust and picked up one of the books. The cover was devoid of any picture but the title was *The Pickwick Papers* by Charles Dickens. "The *Christmas Carol* guy?" Xavier turned the book over in his hand and a large chunk of the middle pages full out. Dust plumed up when the pages landed on the floor. Xavier grimaced and waved his hand in front of his face. He had already had enough of this room.

He checked the batter power on his phone once he was again in the hallway. He still had a charge of 82%. "That would be great if I could get a dammed signal," he said to no one.

He reached the next set of doors and paused. Something farther down the hallway caught his eye. He approached another doorway and shined his phone's meager light on it. The door that was once there was gone. At first Xavier thought it must have rotted and fallen inside the room. In fact, pieces of it lay on the floor just across the threshold, but it did not appear as if the door had rotted away. Something about the pattern of the debris suggested something else.

Something smashed this door down. Something big and strong. Xavier gulped. Before he could stop himself he began imagining the strength required to do such a thing. The hairs on his arms stood up straight again, as if mimicking the soldiers standing at attention outside. *Just find a signal and get out of here*, a voice shouted in his head. *That's enough sightseeing.*

"Got that right," Xavier replied to the voice.

For some reason the air smelled better near the doorway. He stepped inside the room.

It was a boy's bedroom. The years since its last occupant had slept in here could not disguise the fact. Despite its ancient appearance Xavier was reminded of his own room at home. Even the layout was similar, although his room was maybe one-quarter the size. One of the windows was open; a light, steady breeze wafted inside and stirred little dust devils to dance on the pitted hardwood. The boy's bed lay on the floor in front of the window. Xavier approached it.

The air was indeed fresher near the window. Xavier stood in front of it and breathed deeply. He had not realized until that moment the smell of decay and age that had overtaken the house since its...what? Change? No, that wasn't the right word. It wasn't big enough to describe what had happened just as the soldiers showed up outside. After a moment, it came to him. It's *transformation*. His English teacher, Mrs. Gauvin, would be proud of him. *Assuming you see her again*, the voice in his head chimed in. "Shut up," Xavier told it. He was starting to dislike that voice.

He peeked outside. The window looked out on the front yard. From this height he could see the assembled soldiers quite clearly. He could also see Andy and Mr. Bisaillon. The teacher had recovered and now knelt in the tall grass with his hands behind his head, the mirror image of Andy.

He cast a nervous eye at the black birds. They seemed much closer than they had from downstairs. He was able to pick out individual birds in the black mass that maintained that tight circle of darkness in the bright blue sky.

Xavier turned his eyes back to Mr. Bisaillon. He wanted to shout something, anything, to get his teacher's attention. He very nearly did. He stopped himself when it occurred to him he would also draw the attention of the soldiers. The thought of them swinging their rifles toward his window and opening fire killed any thought of trying to shout to Mr. Bisaillon.

Xavier looked at his phone. His lips pursed. He could not do anything to draw the soldiers' attention, but perhaps he was up high enough they would not notice movement in the window. Slowly, expecting the air to erupt in gunfire, Xavier held his phone outside the window. He peeked with one eye at the upper left corner of the screen.

His heart nearly leaped from his chest. The usual message of NO SERVICE was gone, replaced by a single bar. "Oh my God, oh my God," he whispered. Quickly he brought the phone inside and hit the *Recent* icon. The display obediently changed to a list of all the recent numbers he had texted and called. He selected the one labeled MOM and hit it. Nothing happened. No ringing, no elapsed time ticking by. He regarded the phone again. The familiar NO SERVICE message had returned.

Frustrated but not deterred, Xavier again held the phone outside the window.

A high-pitched scream cut through the air. Xavier yelped and jumped back from the window. He felt the phone fly from his fingers and then he was flat on his back. "No!" He scrambled to his feet and all but leaped for the window. He reached it just in time to see his phone disappear into the tall grass below. "No no no *no!*" he shouted.

For an awful moment Xavier pictured himself leaping from the window, following the path of his phone. He could not have lost it, not when he had finally managed to get a signal. He may even have done just that, if not for the soldiers looking up at him and swinging their rifles in his direction.

Xavier cast one long, heartbroken look at the spot where his phone had vanished before he threw himself onto the bed. He curled into a tight ball with his arms covering his head, waiting for the volley of fire to shred the wall next to him.

He did hear several shouts from outside, but the soldiers held their fire. It took several moments for Xavier to realize they were not going to launch a barrage of gunfire in his direction. Slowly, tentatively, he opened up. He dared not look outside again, despite the sudden and continuous clamor that reached his ears. On hands and knees he crawled from the bed. He cast a final look over his shoulder at the window and his lost phone. As he did he bumped into something.

Xavier looked forward. A pair of boots stood directly in front of him. Every muscle in his body froze instantly. *Those boots weren't there a minute ago*, the voice in his head informed him. *No kidding*, Xavier thought back. His eyes moved on their own. They followed the boots up to a pair of blue leggings. Then a black leather belt. On the side of the belt was a long sheath. What could only be a sword handle protruded from that sheath. Xavier's eyes continued their slow climb.

Above the belt was a blue shirt with silver buttons down the center. Two gloved hands hung on either side of the shirt. A single stripe (*a chevron*, the voice informed him, *remember? From Miss DiBella's second marking period history class?*) adorned each sleeve near the shoulder. Atop it all was the face of the man inside the uniform.

Man? A kid, maybe only a year or two older than Xavier. The kid-soldier looked down upon him, his face expressionless.

The world suddenly swam out of focus. Xavier felt his arms buckle and then his cheek rested upon the cold hardwood of a little boy's bedroom. He remembered nothing after that.

Chapter Ten

A New Message, A Betrayal

Carlos ran for the front doors and looked out the windows. There were a lot of gray- and blue-shirted soldiers on the front deck. They were moving off, now, some of the officers shouting orders to them. He could see no sign of Mr. Bisaillon.

"Andy, what happened to Mr. B?" Carlos asked, turning away from the window.

The new arrival was unsteady on his feet, alternately leaning against the wall and Nevaeh. He shook his head every few moments like a cartoon character who had just taken a pounding in the boxing ring. Finally he looked at Carlos, his expression entirely uncomprehending.

"Huh?"

"Mr. Bisaillon! Where is he? What happened out there?"

"He was right behind me."

"Well, he ain't there now," Kyle said, his back still against the door.

Carlos looked at the bigger boy. "You didn't..." His voice trailed off. No, no way. Kyle Reed was a jerk, the biggest jerk in the school and destined for low-paying menial jobs for the rest of his life, yes. But even *he* wasn't capable of that.

"Didn't *what*?" Kyle was back to his usual angry self in an instant.

"Forget it," Carlos told him.

"Damn right, forget it." Kyle stepped away from the door, peeked through the window.

"You okay?" Carlos asked, turning his attention to Andy.

Andy nodded and immediately grimaced. "Head hurts, but yeah, I guess so. Wait a minute. Something happened. Those guys in the Civil War getup looked like they were about to shoot at the house. Then there was a scream. They got distracted and that's when Mr. Bisaillon grabbed one of them. Then we ran for it."

"They must have caught Mr. B," Nevaeh stated matter-of-factly.

"Thanks, Captain Obvious," Kyle remarked.

Nevaeh took an angry step in Kyle's direction. Carlos got between them and stopped her. "We can't fight with each other, not now, anyway. Save it for when we get outta here."

Nevaeh glared at Kyle but the fight seemed to have left her. She turned and walked to Maya. Both girls kept their silence.

"What did you find in the basement?" Carlos asked Kyle. "Anything?"

"Not much, just a lot of old junk," Kyle replied.

"And a big dog," Nevaeh added. When Carlos looked at her questioningly, she continued, "Or something. I don't know what it was. Some kind of animal. I heard it growl."

Carlos glanced at Kyle.

The bigger boy shrugged. "I didn't hear nothin'. We were checking the place out and then she freaked and ran. Left me all alone down there. *Alone* being the important word in that sentence. No wild animals, no nothin'."

"You liar!" Nevaeh shouted. "There *was* an animal or something down there! I heard it!"

"Whatever," Kyle remarked. He kicked at a stray piece of rotted wood on the floor.

"And where's my phone? You had it."

"I dropped it. Maybe that wild animal of yours ate it."

Nevaeh glowered at him. Her mouth worked but she seemed too angry to speak at that moment. Maya placed a comforting hand on her arm.

"We'll get the phone later," Carlos assured the angry girl. "For now I still have mine. And Xavier—" Carlos's eyes widened. "Oh, man, where's Xavier?"

"Probably hiding under a bed somewhere," Kyle sneered.

Carlos craned his neck toward the second floor. "Xavier!" The walls threw echoes of his voice in every direction. Carlos tried again. He could hear nothing from the second floor. "We have to go find him."

"Uh-uh, no way," Nevaeh told him. "I ain't going nowhere. We're waiting right here for someone to come get us." She checked with Maya. The other girl nodded silently.

Carlos's lips pressed into a thin line. "Fine, stay here. Keep a close watch on those guys outside. See if you can spot Mr. Bisaillon. Kyle and I will look for—"

"Whoa, whoa, whoa." Kyle held up both hands. "I don't even like the little jerk. And since when do I take orders from you, Medina? Suddenly you're the teacher now?"

Carlos nearly began another argument but he stopped himself. What was the point? "Okay, you can stay here. With the *girls*. Me and Andy will go upstairs. You game?"

Andy stopped rubbing the back of his head long enough to give Carlos a thumbs-up.

"We'll find Xavier and come right back down," Carlos told Nevaeh and Maya. "Hang tight."

****

Nevaeh watched the two boys ascend the right staircase to the second floor. One of the steps creaked loudly and she was certain it would give way, plunging both boys to who-knew-where. Carlos and Andy sprinted up the last few steps and made it to the second floor landing. Carlos waved. Nevaeh waved back. Then he and Andy were gone from her sight.

Kyle turned to them. "Sorry I dropped your phone. Wanna go find it?" His voice was calm, even soothing, very unKyle-like. Even his expression was soft.

"Are you serious?"

Kyle shrugged. "The only two phones are upstairs now. Wouldn't you feel better if you had yours back?"

She would. Nevaeh glanced at Maya. Her friend looked reluctant, to say the least. "He has a point," Neveah told her. "What if..." She was about to say, *What if they don't come back?* but she stopped herself. "What if I get home and my mom's really mad at me for losing it? She'll ground me for a month."

"Neveah, I don't know..."

"Please!" Nevaeh was surprised at how much she wanted to get her phone back. It had nothing to do with the possibility of being grounded for losing it; she was suddenly convinced she would never see Xavier and the other boys again. This house was going to swallow them up and never spit them out. That meant her phone was the only chance they had left of calling for help. It really was that simple. "Please," she repeated, her tone soft.

Maya looked down the hallway leading to the kitchen. Then at Kyle. Then back to Nevaeh. "Okay, fine. We'll get your phone."

Nevaeh smiled. "Thank you."

Kyle led the way back to the kitchen. There was still plenty of daylight left, judging by the meager light that managed to get through the grime and dust on the windows. Kyle strode to the nearest window and peeked outside. His body language told Nevaeh all she needed to know about what he saw in the back yard.

She took a single step in the direction of the door which led to the basement. She froze when her eyes fell upon the refrigerator. The letter magnets spelled out a different message than before. It read: TH IDOL IS TH K Y.

"What's that mean?" Maya asked when she followed her friend's gaze.

Nevaeh turned to Kyle. "You need to knock that off," she hissed. "Stop trying to scare me!"

Kyle turned away from the window. "What are you talking about?" Some of his usual belligerence had returned to his voice since the foyer.

Nevaeh pointed to the fridge. "That. Stop leaving me your little love notes on the fridge. It ain't funny."

Kyle looked at the refrigerator door and his brow furrowed. He appeared confused but only for a moment. Then he shrugged. "Sorry. Thought I'd play around with ya a little. My bad."

"Just don't do it anymore," Nevaeh told him. She pointed to the basement door. "You gonna go get it or what?"

"*We* are gonna go get it," Kyle replied.

Nevaeh expected as much. "Okay. But you dropped it so you go first. We'll follow you."

"Bunch of wussies around here," Kyle mumbled. He strode to the door purposefully and grasped the handle. He yanked it open quite suddenly and with far more force than was necessary. He peered inside. "See? No wild animals, no monsters, no nothing." He took a step toward the threshold.

He spun so quickly Nevaeh never saw it coming. The large boy grabbed Maya's arm and threw her toward the open door. The girl screamed and disappeared into the darkness. Nevaeh heard the unmistakable sound of her friend tumbling down the steps. "*Maya!*" Nevaeh ran to the open door.

Rough hands planted themselves on her back and shoved. Nevaeh lost all semblance of balance. Her hand brushed against the rail but only for a split-second, not long enough for her to grab it. She hit the first step, then the second, each impact sending lightning bolts throughout her body. She fell for what seemed like hours until she finally came to a stop at the bottom of the stairs. She had landed on something soft; it took her only a moment to realize it was her friend.

"Maya? You okay?"

A weak whimper, barely audible, was the only reply she received.

"Someone wants to meet you," she heard Kyle say from somewhere far away.

Nevaeh looked up the stairs. Kyle stood silhouetted in the doorway. She could not see his face but she knew he was smiling.

"Have fun!" He slammed the door closed.

The darkness of the basement became absolute. Nevaeh felt about until she found the first step. Before she could even attempt the stairs she had to extricate herself from Maya. Her friend had yet to say anything. Nevaeh did not know if the girl was even conscious.

"Such sweet, pretty little girls," a woman's voice purred from the darkness.

Every muscle in Nevaeh's body locked up. Unable to move, unable to speak, her eyes turned in the direction of the voice. She could see nothing, of course, but she knew whomever was down here with them was coming closer. She thought she could hear footsteps drawing closer to her, but it might have been her own heartbeat. It thundered in her ears and threatened to drown out all other sound in the world.

The basement had gotten colder since she had ventured down here with Kyle. It seemed to radiate from the floor, the walls, everything. She told herself it was for this reason alone her muscles began to quiver.

Then, quite suddenly, she could see something. *Two* somethings, it turned out. They were small and red and they were definitely approaching her. And still she could not move a muscle.

The two red somethings became a pair of eyes. They emerged from the darkness of the basement, becoming brighter as their owner drew closer. The woman knelt in the dirt next to the two girls. Nevaeh felt the woman's hand beneath her chin, lifting up her head as if to get a better look at her. Nevaeh recoiled and gasped at the woman's frigid touch. The hand may as well have been sculpted from ice. Her chin went numb immediately.

"Very pretty indeed." Her voice was soft velvet, like a movie star's from the 1940s. "And I have so many things to show you."

The woman stood. Somehow, despite the complete darkness, Nevaeh knew the woman had spread her arms wide. She also became aware that the woman was not alone. There was someone else down here. Or some*thing*. And it was big.

"Help them to their feet," the woman ordered.

Something that felt very much like the paw of a giant animal settled under Nevaeh's arm. She felt herself being lifted into the air.

Nevaeh found her voice at last. She screamed.

Chapter Eleven

The Messengers, Andy Takes A Spill

"Did you hear that?"

Carlos paused in the hallway. He and Andy had just exited the third room in their so-far-fruitless search for Xavier.

"Hear what?"

"Shh!" Carlos held up his hand and listened intently. Aside from his own breathing he could hear nothing. He shook his head. "I don't know. I thought I heard something from downstairs. Then again, it might have been from outside, too. This house does something weird to sounds."

"I didn't hear anything," Andy told him.

Carlos shook his head again. "It was probably nothing. Let's keep going."

The next door was locked. Carlos was about to knock, stopped himself. *That would be ridiculous*, he thought. Instead, he shouted, "Xavier? You in there?" He put his ear to the door but no sound came from the other side. He looked at Andy. "You're bigger. See if you can get it open."

Andy appeared reluctant. "You sure about that?"

"Yes," Carlos lied. In point of fact he was not sure he wanted to see the room on the other side of the door.

But it was possible Xavier ran inside and locked it behind him. *Especially if something was chasing him.* "Give it a try."

Andy turned the doorknob. When that didn't produce any results he threw his shoulder into the door. Dust drifted down from the top of the doorframe. The bigger boy coughed and waved it away. He stepped back, then charged at the obstinate door. The wood cracked but the door held. Andy bounced a few feet back. He rubbed his shoulder, looked at Carlos. "Well, that's not opening."

Carlos frowned. "Let's try it together."

The two boys walked back to the opposite wall. They each cast a sideways glance at the other. Then they surged forward.

This time the door shattered under their combined assault. The boys' momentum carried them into the room. Their legs became entangled with one another's and they sprawled onto the floor. The breath exploded from Carlos's lungs. He gasped air, tried to separate himself from his classmate. It took him only a moment and he rolled clear of Andy. He came up sputtering for breath.

His hands and arms were scraped. Pinpricks of blood blossomed on his palms. He rubbed them absently on his pants. When he saw what was in front of him, his breath hitched in his throat and his muscles froze.

Two children stood in front of him and Andy. They were clearly brother and sister. The boy looked to be no more than a year or two younger than Carlos, while the girl was a few years younger than her brother. They did not move, did not speak. They simply looked at the two new arrivals, their expressions blank.

"Who...Who..." Carlos found he could not speak.

"Whoa!" Andy had finally noticed the two kids. He scrambled backwards on his hands and knees toward the now-open doorway. "Carlos! Let's go!"

Carlos found he still could not move. He looked at the kids and they looked at him.

The idol, the boy said without moving his lips. *The idol is the key*.

The little girl appeared to stiffen when her brother spoke. She looked about nervously and tugged on his arm.

Find the idol, the boy continued.

The girl became more frantic. Her eyes flitted about every corner of the room as if she was expecting something bad to happen. *Shawn*, she pleaded. Like her brother she spoke without moving her lips.

"Come on, man, let's go!" Andy shouted from just outside the room.

Carlos realized he had regained some of his ability to move. He glanced over his shoulder at Andy. Just as quickly he whipped his head back to the two children.

They were gone. Carlos was alone inside the room. He looked about but there was nothing within the room that was large enough for two children to hide behind. Not that they could have moved more than a foot or two in the time his head was turned.

Where are their footprints? Carlos gasped. The dust on the floor where the children stood was undisturbed. He looked at the floor around him for confirmation. He had left easily visible footprints in the dust. The two younger kids had not.

"What just happened?" he asked when his voice returned from its brief vacation. "You did see them, right?"

"Oh, I saw them," Andy replied from the hallway. "Can we go now?"

Carlos got to his feet and looked about the room again, as if his eyes deceived him and the two kids were still there. But they were not. He swallowed hard and joined Andy in the hallway. "Let's find Xavier and get back to the others."

Carlos glanced down the hallway and counted doors. "Three more...No, wait. That one at the end, it doesn't have a door. Let's try that one."

Before the two boys could take a step they heard Kyle from downstairs shout, "Hey, morons! Get down here. Nevaeh got hurt. She needs your help!"

Carlos and Andy exchanged glances. As much as Carlos needed to find Xavier he could not ignore Nevaeh if she was hurt. Carlos read Andy's eyes and knew his friend had reached the same conclusion. The two kids who disappeared in front of him temporarily forgotten, Carlos said, "Come on!" They took off back the way they had come.

They took the stairs two at a time despite the groans they received from the decayed wood. Kyle stood in the foyer watching their progress.

"What happened?" Andy asked when they reached the bottom.

"How do I Know?" Kyle replied. "The idiot probably tripped over something in the basement when we were looking for her phone. Can't see much of anything down there. But she's hurt pretty bad."

Andy set off down the hallway which led to the kitchen. Kyle followed him. Carlos remained in the foyer a moment, watching them. Something wasn't right, he didn't know what. It was about Nevaeh and Kyle, that much he knew, but he couldn't figure it out. Whatever it was it remained annoyingly out of his reach, like an itch he simply couldn't scratch. With a frown he followed the other two boys into the kitchen.

When he arrived Kyle had taken position to the side of the basement door, pointing. Andy stood at the threshold, looking down into darkness.

"Nevaeh? Maya? Where are you?"

"I already told you, dummy. They're down there."

Andy frowned at Kyle. He returned his attention to the basement. "Nevaeh? Can you hear me? You okay?"

"They're as okay as they're gonna be," Kyle told him. Then he shoved Andy through the opening.

Carlos rushed forward. He could hear Andy tumbling down the stairs, hear the boy's grunts of pain, and then a crash as he must have hit the bottom.

"Andy!" Carlos had every intention of going after him. In his haste he forgot about Kyle.

The larger boy slammed his elbow into Carlos's stomach. Carlos gulped and doubled over. Kyle threw the basement door shut and turned in his direction. Carlos dropped to one knee. He pushed himself back as the other boy advanced on him. He gulped air, blinked the tears from his eyes.

"Where's..." He found it difficult to speak.

"Nevaeh?" Kyle replied. "Who cares? She's down there somewhere. So is Maya. I suspect Andy will be seeing them real soon. You will, too. And then Valsaint. I can't wait to get my hands on him."

Carlos continued to push himself backward. He felt something behind him. It was the fallen refrigerator. He froze when he saw the letter magnets arranged into a sentence: FIND TH IDOL.

Kyle loomed over him. Both hands were curled into fists. "She said she wants all of you. If I help her she'll let me go." He knelt down until he was eye-level with Carlos. "That's a hell of a deal if you ask me."

Carlos's hand found the refrigerator door handle. It was an inch or two above the floor and hanging from the door by a single screw. He grasped it and hoped it would hold.

"Oh, and you were right, before. Bisaillon almost made it inside. I slammed the door in his face and it felt *awesome*! I wanted to do something like that all year!" Kyle threw his head back and laughed. "Let those Civil War actors outside have him. I think *she* prefers kids, anyway." He ruffled Carlos's hair. "Time to say good night, Medina."

"Good night." Carlos lifted the refrigerator door with everything he had, gasping at the pain it produced in his abdomen. The thing flew open and up. It caught Kyle squarely in the jaw and sent the larger boy stumbling backward. The letter magnets sailed through the air in all directions. Kyle crashed into the counter and bounced off. He landed hard on the floor and rolled.

Carlos pushed himself to his feet. Still holding a hand over his bruised abdomen he staggered from the kitchen. He dropped to one knee a few feet from the foyer, gasping. He could hear Kyle moaning and swearing in the kitchen and knew it would be only a few moments before

James Buchannan Middle School's Bully Number One would be on him again. That thought alone was enough to get Carlos back on his feet. There were certain things all kids knew not to do to live a long, healthy life. Hitting Kyle Reed in the face with a refrigerator door was pretty high on that list. In fact, right now, it was at the top.

Carlos emerged into the foyer, intending to get back up to the second floor. If he could find Xavier before Kyle found him, the two of them together might be enough to handle the bigger boy.

He cast a glance over his shoulder, expecting to see Kyle rocketing up the hallway. As yet there was no sign of him. That was good. Carlos needed as much of a head start as possible. He turned back toward the twin staircases...

And ran directly into Xavier.

Chapter Twelve

Xavier Learns A Few Things

The kid in the blue military uniform extended his hand. Xavier swallowed. The last thing in the world he wanted to do was accept that hand. It would mean touching the kid, and Xavier doubted he would find that a pleasant experience. He eyed the rifle slung over the kid's shoulder. *Well, that pretty much eliminates the possibility of running away*, he thought. Seeing no other option, Xavier accepted the offered hand. It was cold but not as cold as Xavier expected. The kid soldier pulled him to his feet and then stood back.

"You're a ghost, right?" Xavier asked the boy.

A spirit, yes, the kid said without moving his lips. He snapped off a salute. *Private Caleb Mason, at your service, sir.*

"Nice to meet you." It was all Xavier could think to say.

You and your friends are in very serious trouble, I'm afraid, Caleb continued, still without moving his lips. *In fact, I'd say you've never been in this much trouble in your whole life.*

Xavier rubbed the back of his neck. "We're trapped in a house that's surrounded by some weird army guys and we can't call for help. So, yeah, we're in trouble."

Caleb smirked and nodded. *But that's not the worst of it. If you ever want to see your family again you have to know what's happening, and what came before. I can show you, if you'll let me.*

Xavier took an involuntary step back. Although this kid had done him no harm, and seemed decidedly non-hostile, by his own admission he was a ghost. That meant he was dead. *Then again, with everything that's happened today, is* this *where you draw the line?* Xavier willed the voice in his head to shut up. He was not comforted by the idea that the voice was right.

"I guess," he said at last.

Caleb extended his hand again. Xavier looked at it again, quite skeptically, then slowly placed his hand in the dead boy's.

There was a *whoosh* and Xavier felt the bile rising up in his throat. It was similar to the sensation he received when the house transformed around them. The world whipped past him far too quickly for him to see anything other than a blur. There was sound, as well, a cacophony that assaulted his ears even after he covered them with his hands. The rollercoaster feeling returned, much more powerful than it had been earlier. This time Xavier felt he was close to losing consciousness. He wanted to tell Caleb to stop but his voice died in his throat. Or perhaps he was screaming at the top of his lungs. There was no way to know.

And then the world slammed back into focus. Xavier gasped for breath, afraid to lift his head or even open his eyes. He was outside someplace; the dirt and grass beneath him told him that much. The sound that had filled his world only a moment before was gone, replaced with shouts and cries and the unmistakable crack of gunshots. Xavier shook his head to clear it. Slowly, with the utmost reluctance, he opened his eyes.

He found himself in the middle of a battle. Soldiers in blue uniforms fought others wearing gray. Some fought hand-to-hand, some swung their rifles at each other, but most were firing their weapons at the enemy. Men and boys fell all around him. No, not him, *them*. Caleb surveyed the battle, a curiously detached expression etched into his features. After a few moments he seemed to remember Xavier was next to him. Again, he offered his hand. This time Xavier waved him off and stood on his own. Touching the boy soldier twice was more than enough for Xavier. He looked about.

The battle was not going well for the blue coats. Xavier saw many of them, most of them, lying about the ground. A few struggled weakly to crawl away but most were still as statues. The gray coats were firing their rifles and surging forward. Although he could hear their rifle shots as well as the screams of the dying, he could smell nothing. He felt he should be grateful for that.

That these men and boys were dressed identically to the soldiers presently holding Mr. Bisaillon and Andy at the business end of their rifles was not lost on Xavier.

Here we come, Caleb informed him. When Xavier gave him a confused look, Caleb pointed down the hill.

One of the blue coats was running in their direction, being pulled by his arm by a very large Indian man with a bear claw instead of a right hand. As they drew nearer, Xavier gasped in surprise. The blue coat was Caleb. He did not know the boy's companion but his mind suddenly flashed back to the thing he had glimpsed in the woods as they walked along the driveway. Although he did not know how, Xavier knew this was what he had seen in the shadows, stalking them.

I never knew his real name. Or maybe it really was Black Bear. Let's follow them, Caleb suggested.

Not seeing as he had a choice, Xavier followed the ghost.

Caleb—the *live* Caleb—and his very large companion stopped running when they crested the hill. The Indian knelt and rummaged through his satchel. Caleb swung his rifle up and aimed it back the way they had come. As yet the gray coats were busying themselves with whoever remained of their enemy but the boy's expression told Xavier he knew what was coming.

Xavier's eyes were drawn to the Indian. His hand emerged from his satchel with something roughly the size of a bowling ball, although it was not round. It was black, the darkest shade of black Xavier had ever seen. He could not make out what it was, although something about it suggested the form of a bird.

The Indian used his bear claw to tear up the ground. Dirt flew in all directions. Some of it passed through Xavier's body as if he himself were a ghost. When Black Bear was satisfied with the size and depth of the hole he placed the black thing inside it and mumbled something Xavier could not hear.

The gray coats were charging up the hill toward them. Black Bear stood and hurled himself at them. Live-Caleb stood, apparently as stunned as was Xavier, at the Indian's savage attack. The gray coats seemed unable to aim their weapons at him, so swiftly did he move. Eventually, however, their numbers won out and Black Bear disappeared beneath a crushing wave of gray uniforms.

Look, ghost-Caleb told him, and pointed.

Xavier looked.

At first he thought it was smoke. Something poured from the hole Black Bear had dug into the earth. The smoke expanded and thickened until Xavier could not see through it. Something moved within the smoke, within the *darkness*. Xavier thought it was a woman, although something about her also reminded him of a bird. What could only have been her eyes snapped open. They were bright red and focused on the men still struggling with

Black Bear. The woman and her accompanying zone of darkness surged past Xavier and ghost-Caleb, directly into the mass of soldiers.

At the same time the sky suddenly darkened. Xavier's eyes were drawn upward. Black birds, thousands of them, surged through the air as if they were a single animal. They moved so quickly toward the gray coats Xavier imagined he could feel the wind generated by their flight.

She is Tah-tah-Kro'-ah, *the raven queen, although I did not know it at the time,* ghost-Caleb told him. *She is the last of five sisters who once roamed this world. The natives both worshipped and feared them.* He indicated the soldiers with a nod of his head. *She did what she and her sisters have done since the world was new. She took them all, those who were still living, anyway. This part you probably don't need to see.* He placed his hand over Xavier's eyes.

At first Xavier struggled to get rid of the dead boy's hand, but after a moment of listening to the screams of the surprised soldiers, he decided Caleb was right. He most definitely did not need to see this.

When Caleb lowered his hand Xavier saw all of the gray coats were down. The woman knelt in the dirt beside Black Bear. She seemed to be speaking to him. After a moment the big Indian rose to his feet. He bled from a number of wounds but he seemed unbothered by them. His eyes, too, were red, although they lacked the intensity of the woman's. He began to stride back up the hill, toward live-Caleb.

Xavier turned quickly to his companion. "What is he doing?"

You don't need to see this, either, ghost-Caleb told him.

And then the world spun out of focus and Xavier was back aboard the rollercoaster again.

This time the sensation of being weightless and whipping through space was shorter, although just as violent and unsettling. The sudden stop sent Xavier sprawling onto a hard surface.

"There has to be a better way of doing this," he mumbled. He pushed himself to his knees, willing his stomach to settle down, and looked about.

He was back inside the house, in the living room. The room itself had changed since he last saw it. The furniture was new and clean, the walls adorned with some family photos and paintings. Xavier could hear crickets chirping in the darkness outside.

A woman sat in one of the chairs. A single candle next to her provided the only light within the room but somehow Xavier could see everything quite clearly. She sat and knitted but something about her movements made him uneasy. They were precise, robotic, as if her mind were a million miles away.

Her name was Mrs. Meijer, Caleb informed him. *Her husband built the house in 1881. He passed away a few years later, leaving her to raise their three boys alone.*

At the mention of children Xavier realized he could hear them playing upstairs. Or perhaps not playing. What he took at first to be playful shouting now sounded more like panic. He looked again at Mrs. Meijer. "Something's wrong. Doesn't she hear them?"

Caleb shrugged. *I suppose, on some level. But the raven queen has a way of clouding the senses of adults. They hear, but they don't hear. See, but not see.*

"They're in trouble!" Xavier exclaimed. He made for the staircase, but stopped short when Caleb appeared suddenly in front of him.

I would spare you what lies upstairs.

More sounds from the three Meijer children. Xavier was close enough now that he knew those were not the sounds of play. Something very bad was happening on the second floor. He tried to run through the ghost-boy but Caleb was solid enough that Xavier could not get past him.

"We have to help them!"

We cannot. What you're hearing happened before your great-grandfather was born. It cannot be altered by any means we possess.

Xavier tried again to shoulder his way past Caleb, and again he was unsuccessful. In frustration he turned back toward the living room. "Why isn't she doing something? Is she deaf?"

I told you, she is aware of what's happening, but that realization is buried deep down inside of her. She cannot help her sons. He sounded both sad and resigned.

From upstairs Xavier could hear a woman's voice. It was soft and thick, like poisoned honey. "I have such things to show you," the voice said.

Xavier swallowed hard. "You were right. I don't want to see this."

Caleb placed his hand on Xavier's arm. The room blurred and they were flying again.

When he landed this time he found himself in the room where his journey with Caleb began. They were still in the past, judging by the near-pristine condition of the room.

Two children stood by the window. The older of the two, a boy, looked down, as if judging the distance to the ground below. His younger sister sat on the bed and cried. Something pounded on the door, something *big* from the sound of it. Xavier could guess what it was.

This is Shawn and Maureen Sullivan, Caleb told him.

"And we can't help them, either." It was not a question. He turned quickly on Caleb. "Why are you showing me all this if we can't do anything to help them?"

Because it can help you and your friends, the ghost replied.

The door exploded and sent splinters flying throughout the room. Instinctively Xavier shielded himself before he remembered the splinters could not harm him. The shadowy bulk of Black Bear stood silhouetted within the doorframe. The Sullivan children screamed.

"Get me out of here," Xavier stated flatly. "I don't want to see any more."

Caleb looked at him, nodded once.

The bedroom and the Sullivan children vanished. When Xavier next opened his eyes he was back inside the room. He was no longer in the past; a single look about what was once Shawn Sullivan's bedroom told him they were back in the present. Caleb stood silently next to him.

"So now what?" Xavier asked.

The idol that summoned the raven queen still lies where Black Bear buried it, Caleb replied. *If you ever wish to see your family again you must destroy it.*

"Oh, is that all?" Xavier was too tired to keep the desperation out of his tone. "And how do I do that, exactly?"

To destroy a spectral object you need a spectral weapon.

"Okay, I'll just run down to Target. Be right back."

I fear I do not know what that means, Caleb replied. *But there is something within this house you can use.*

Xavier snapped his fingers. "Your rifle!"

Caleb shook his head. *It is as non-corporeal as am I. You need something that exists in this world, not the spirit world.*

Now it was Xavier's turn to shake his head. "I don't know. I just don't know."

Caleb said, *I can tell you but you will not like it.*

Xavier threw his hands in the air. "Go ahead, tell me."

Caleb told him.

Xavier did not like it.

Chapter Thirteen

Xavier Meets the Raven Queen

"Xavier! Where the heck have you been? We looked all over for you!"

Carlos nearly hugged him. He restrained himself when he remembered who was likely to join them in the foyer at any moment. He cast a quick glance over his shoulder toward the kitchen but Kyle had yet to show himself.

"We have to hide! Reed threw Andy into the cellar. I think he did the same thing to the girls, too. He's working with whatever is creeping around down there. And he'll be here any second."

Xavier waved him off. "Listen, I have a plan to get us out of this, but you have to do what I say."

Hope, the first real hope Carlos felt since the house changed around them, flashed across his eyes. "Okay, what is it?"

Xavier told him as much of what he learned as he felt Carlos would believe. He made no mention of Caleb and shied away from questions about the Sullivan kids. He ended with, "Keep Reed busy. Get him as far from the basement as you can."

Carlos' face fell. "You're kidding."

"No time to argue. Do it!"

Carlos thought this was the perfect time to argue. He opened his mouth to do just that when he heard Kyle Reed curse loudly from down the hallway. "Whatever you're gonna do, do it fast, Valsaint."

Xavier nodded and ducked into the ruins of the study.

Carlos stood at the bottom of the staircase and peeked around the corner. Kyle was coming up the hallway. The larger boy was rubbing his chin and spitting on the floor as he stumbled toward him. "You're a dead man, Medina! Wait'll I get my hands on you!"

Carlos ascended the stairs until he was about halfway to the second floor. He stopped and looked back down. Kyle had reached the foyer. He looked about, his eyes lingering on the open doorway to the study. He took a step in that direction.

Carlos licked his lips. He was about to do the single dumbest thing he had ever done in his life and he knew it. *Xavier's plan better work*, he thought, and shouted,

"Hey, genius, I'm up here!"

Kyle whirled. His eyes fixed on Carlos and his lips spread into a hungry grin. Blood dripped from his nose and he sniffled it back. "Time to pay the piper," Kyle said with glee.

"Come and get me." Carlos bolted the rest of the way up the stairs. He chose the hallway on the right, lingering just long enough for Kyle to see which way he went. Then he was running as fast as he could.

*****

Xavier heard Kyle race up the stairs, not even pausing at the collapsed area in his quest for vengeance against Carlos Medina. He hated to turn his friend into a moving target but what he had to do would be difficult enough without Kyle Reed trying to stop him. He just hoped Carlos would be able to stay ahead of the bigger boy long enough for Xavier to follow Caleb's instructions.

Xavier raced down the hallway and into the kitchen. He stopped short when he saw Shawn and Maureen Sullivan. The two siblings knelt on the floor in front of the refrigerator. They were picking up the scattered letter magnets and arranging them into a message on the refrigerator door. They had gotten as far as: FIND TH

Xavier nodded. "The idol, I know."

The two children continued with their task as if he had not spoken, although the little girl favored him with a smile. Xavier smiled back and waved. Then he turned his attention to the basement door.

The last thing in the world he wanted to do was go through that door. Nonetheless he placed his hand on the knob and turned. The door opened easily enough. He peered down the steps and called out, "Andy? You guys down there?"

At first he heard nothing. Then, a soft sobbing. It sounded distant, as if he were listening to the anguish of someone long dead. Xavier swallowed and then took a deep breath. He could not put this off any longer. He thought of Carlos, running around upstairs with an enraged Kyle Reed after him. That more than anything got him moving.

The first step was missing. He stepped over it gently and slowly. The rest of the steps creaked and sagged beneath his weight but they held. He became aware that the temperature seemed to drop more with each step he took into the basement. The bottom step groaned so loudly Xavier's heart almost stopped. *Get a grip*, he told himself. *It's not like you're about to do something incredibly stupid.* Xavier left the steps behind and turned the corner.

The temperature in the basement was polar. Xavier would not have been overly surprised had the place been covered in ice and snow. He took a slow, deep breath, felt the cold air invade his lungs. He shivered, just a little, but enough for anyone watching him to notice.

Andy, Navaeh and Maya knelt in the center of the basement. The sobs he heard were coming from Maya but the other two looked as scared as did she, as scared as Xavier himself. Each child shivered and their teeth chattered. They shook as if they were sitting atop a live electrical wire. They looked at him with wide, wet, pleading eyes. Xavier took another deep breath. He wanted to say something, say anything that would reassure them. He found he could no longer speak. He merely nodded to them and hoped that would be enough.

The zone of darkness he had first seen erupt from the ground on a Civil War battlefield blocked his view of everything on the far side of his kneeling classmates. Something moved within that darkness. A pair of red eyes blazed at him. A woman's voice seemed to come from all around the basement.

"Come, my child," Tah-tah-Kro'-ah purred. "Join your friends."

Xavier inched closer to the darkness. "I know what you are," he said. He paused when he realized his voice had returned. *Better keep going before it disappears on you again*, he thought. *And next time it might not come back at all*. He swallowed again. "You're the raven queen."

Tah-tah-Kro'-ah laughed. It was the sound of something heavy being dragged across crushed glass. "Indeed," she replied when the laughter ended.

"Andy, I'm gonna need your help," Xavier said. Andy did not reply. He blinked his wet eyes at Xavier.

Something big moved around from behind the raven queen and stood slightly in front of her, directly behind the three kneeling children. Black Bear's eyes—not quite as brilliant as the woman-thing's—seemed to drill into

Xavier's head. Xavier blinked away the slight pain that worked its way into his skull.

His eyes focused on the bear claw that served as the warrior's right hand. Xavier licked his dry lips and took a step back. "I know who you are, too, Black Bear. And I know what you did. Caleb Mason sends his regards."

Black Bear roared as loudly as a real bear. Xavier turned and bolted up the stairs. He could hear the big warrior's heavy footfalls coming after him.

He reached the kitchen and saw the two children were gone. They had stuck around long enough to leave another message. D STROY TH IDOL

"Working on it," Xavier replied to the now-vanished siblings.

He slammed the basement door closed just as Black Bear reached the threshold. The door shuddered in its frame and dust drifted down from the ceiling. Xavier heard the Native American warrior grunt and then another impact shook the door. Plaster joined the dust this time. It pattered onto the kitchen floor. Xavier backed up.

The door shattered like glass under the next impact. Rotted wood flew in all directions. Xavier shielded his eyes, felt the splinters sting his hands and his arms. Black Bear entered the kitchen.

Xavier turned toward the back door. He stopped dead in his tracks when he saw a pool of what looked like black smoke seep through the cracks in the linoleum and swirl around his feet. The temperature in the kitchen plummeted, raising the gooseflesh on Xavier's arms. The black smoke expanded and rose and became the raven queen. She floated a few inches above the floor, directly in front of Xavier. Her red eyes snapped open.

Xavier could see some of the woman-thing's features. Her mouth was elongated and wide and resembled a bird's beak. *Except no bird has teeth like that*, some part of his mind informed him. Those teeth were long and sharp, more like the fangs of a snake. If she had a nose it was small enough that Xavier could not see it. Her eyes were deeply set and focused squarely on him.

She extended her arms—or maybe they were wings— and wrapped them around Xavier's body. The temperature dropped even more within her embrace and now Xavier's breath frosted the air.

"Do not struggle, child," she whispered into his ear. "You will enjoy what I have to show you."

Despite his best efforts tears began to flow from Xavier's eyes. They froze on his skin.

Chapter Fourteen

Xavier Gets Some Fresh Air

"Where you at, Medina? You can't hide from me forever, you know."

Carlos listened with his ear to the door. He guessed Kyle was maybe fifteen feet farther up the hallway, and he was coming closer. One more room to check, maybe two, and Kyle would be on him. It was blind luck Carlos had chosen this room; there was a side door which led to another room. Carlos had opened it and peeked inside and saw what he took to be a sewing room. It gave him a way out if (*when*) Kyle finally found him.

"I give you and Valsaint to the woman, she lets me go," Kyle said. "Where is that little weasel, anyway? He hiding with you?" The sound of a door opening, a pause, then, "I sure hope so. I wanna wrap this up and get home in time for dinner."

Carlos backed away from the door as silently as he could. He tiptoed across the room and stood by the other door. He turned the knob, winced as it produced a squeak. His eyes darted back to where he had been standing.

"Little pigs, little pigs, let me in," Kyle called from the other side of the door. "I heard that, you idiots."

Carlos watched the door handle turn. He was through the other door in an instant. He closed it behind him and looked about. The sewing room contained several mannequins in various states of dress. The ancient fabric which clung to their frames was moth-eaten and covered with dust and cobwebs. A small table still stood near the window. The sewing machine which sat atop the table was old and looked as if it were made of cast iron. The door which led to the hallway stood against the far wall. Carlos started for it.

The floor groaned and buckled beneath his feet. The loud *crack* of wood breaking echoed loudly within the room. Carlos yelped and threw himself back. The floor did not give way but he knew he had come close to going through.

Kyle knocked on the side door. "Stop making this harder than it has to be, Medina."

Carlos scrambled to his feet. He eyed the weak spot in the floor and carefully but quickly made his way around it.

The door flew open and Kyle stepped inside the sewing room. "Hey, Medina. How's it going?" His tone was friendly, even conversational, as if he were seeing an old friend for the first time in years. He slammed his fist into his open palm and glanced about the room. "Valsaint in here somewhere?"

Carlos did not reply. He backed slowly toward the door.

Kyle closed the side door behind him and smiled. "Guess not. That's okay, I'll find him. Or she will."

Carlos put his back to the door.

Kyle advanced on him slowly, his smile still in place. "I'm gonna enjoy the hell out of this."

Kyle's foot found the soft spot on the floor. The wood creaked loudly. With a loud, sharp *crack*, the floor gave way. Kyle yelped and threw his arms out. He managed to catch himself while his upper body was still inside the room. He struggled against the rotting wood but it seemed he was stuck. The uneven, broken edges of the floorboards dug into his skin and tore at his shirt every time he tried to pull himself back up. He cursed and flailed his arms wildly.

"Not as much as I enjoyed that," Carlos finally replied. He opened the door and stepped through.

"We ain't done yet, Medina! As soon as I get outta here you're dead! You hear me? *Dead!*"

"They heard you in Pittsburgh," Carlos said, but he was already back in the hallway and heading for the stairs so Kyle did not hear him.

*****

Xavier's vision started to blur. The edges were growing dark and that darkness was spreading. He struggled against the raven queen's embrace but he was simply not strong enough to break free.

"He is magnificent, isn't he?" she whispered into his ear.

At first he had no idea about whom she was speaking. Then his worsening vision beheld Black Bear. Xavier had actually forgotten his presence. The big warrior made his way slowly across the kitchen in their direction. He raised his giant bear paw. The weakening sunlight from outside glinted off the sharp claws. Xavier closed his eyes.

There was a roar from in front of him. Xavier braced for the impact of those claws on his flesh. Instead he heard a second roar, this one unmistakably from Black Bear. It sounded surprised and angry. Xavier opened one eye and squinted.

Andy clung to Black Bear's back. The boy's left arm was wrapped around Black Bear's neck while his right rained blows on the ancient warrior's bare chest. Black Bear spun about so quickly Andy's legs shot out and he looked, for the briefest of moments, like a trapeze artist in mid-air

"Get the claw! Get the claw!" Xavier shouted.

Andy did not even have time to look at him. Black Bear spun around again and this time Andy lost his grip. He sailed through the air and crashed into the cabinets.

The wood splintered and Andy landed on the counter before rolling onto the floor. He groaned but did not move again.

Before Xavier had time to be disappointed it was Nevaeh's turn to leap onto Black Bear's back. Black Bear grunted and flailed at the young girl. That was when Xavier saw Maya take a hesitant step into the kitchen. She was terrified, obviously, and tears streamed freely down her cheeks. Her eyes were focused on her friend and she screamed Nevaeh's name.

It took only a moment for Black Bear to rid himself of the girl. He shrugged his broad shoulders and Nevaeh fell and landed hard on her back. Maya took a single step toward her but froze when Black Bear turned in her direction.

"Leave them alone!" Xavier shouted. Or he might have said nothing. The cold from the raven queen had by now seeped into his bones and his vision was turning black.

"Such spirited little children," Tah-tah-Kro'-ah said. She sounded quite pleased, even proud of them. "Delicious."

Xavier felt himself falling. He landed on the cold kitchen floor and lay there in a heap of quivering muscles. He got the impression the raven queen was moving away from him but he could see nothing. *Sorry, Caleb*, he thought. *I tried*.

*****

Carlos reached the foyer. He heard commotion coming from the kitchen and headed in that direction. As he neared the threshold he stopped and hugged the wall. Shouts. Sounds of things breaking. Grunts that sounded as if they came from a wild animal. He shivered at the sudden drop in temperature. Steeling himself, he inched closer and peered into the kitchen.

It was chaos. Xavier and Nevaeh were down. Maya knelt beside her friend and shook her. Andy lay on the floor near the counter and pushed himself to his knees. The man Xavier described before sending Carlos upstairs loomed above them all. But it was the woman who drew and held Carlos's gaze. Her arms were spread wide as if to encompass the entire room. The darkness around her seemed to form the shape of wings.

Carlos looked again at Xavier. His friend was awake and looked at him with pleading eyes. He said something but it was a croak and Carlos could not hear him. So Xavier pointed at the bird woman. Carlos nodded and looked about frantically. Pieces of broken dishes from the kitchen littered the hallway. He scooped up the biggest piece he could find. Carlos took a deep breath to steady himself. Then he stepped into the doorway and threw the broken dish as hard as he could at the woman.

It vanished into the darkness surrounding her but it must have made contact. She whirled in his direction. Red eyes narrowed as she beheld the small boy in the doorway.

Carlos found himself rooted to the spot. As much as he wanted to turn and run his feet felt as if they had been bolted to the floor. The woman glided across the kitchen in his direction.

That was when Xavier made his move.

*****

Xavier willed his muscles to move. Despite the cold, despite the numbness in his limbs, he managed to regain his feet. He needed a moment, just one, to steady himself, but there was no time. With a roar, he threw himself at Black Bear.

The giant warrior was unprepared for such a move. Xavier crashed into him and their momentum carried them toward the back door. Just as Xavier thought they would make it Black Bear bore down and stopped them inches from the target. Xavier's eyes moved up slowly. Black Bear glared at him, his red eyes ablaze with anger. Xavier gulped.

Something heavy crashed into Xavier's back and once again they were moving forward. This time Black Bear could not stop them. They smashed through the back door and suddenly Xavier was outside the house. He landed atop Black Bear but that lasted only a moment. Xavier tumbled off and rolled away. He gulped air; even given his present situation his mind registered how clean and fresh the air smelled. He had not realized until that moment how thick with decay the air inside the house had been. Absently he registered the sudden increase in temperature. It felt sixty degrees warmer outside then it had in the kitchen.

Xavier rolled onto his stomach and pushed himself to his knees. Andy sat atop Black Bear, struggling with the big Indian. *So it was Andy who crashed into us*, Xavier thought. He silently thanked his friend. As Xavier got back on his feet Andy finally lost the battle. Black Bear rolled and wound up on top of the boy. He raised his bear paw. Andy held his arms in front of him and screamed.

Xavier moved.

Chapter Fifteen

Tah-tah-Kro'-ah

Black Bear roared. The giant bear paw descended, its claws slicing the air.

Xavier grasped it with both hands. The sheer strength of the ancient warrior's arm carried Xavier forward and down. His feet left the ground and for a moment he was airborne. Then he slammed onto the hard earth. The breath exploded from his lungs and stars danced across his vision.

He expected to hear Andy scream as those claws cut through him but the scream never came. Xavier rolled onto his stomach and looked at his friend.

Andy was still down, still holding his arms out in front of him to ward off the blow, but it was no longer necessary. Black Bear still knelt atop the boy but there was something different about him. His right arm ended at his elbow. He stared at the stump with genuine astonishment. It was at that moment Xavier realized he had the bear paw in his hands.

Black Bear looked at the empty space that used to be both his limb and his primary weapon. His gaze shifted slowly to Xavier.

Well, I'm about to die, Xavier thought.

Black Bear threw back his head and roared silently into the twilight sky. The wind picked up and whipped through his long hair. His body quivered. As Xavier watched, the ancient warrior's skin turned gray. Flakes fell off and were borne away by the wind. In seconds he was no more than a small dust cloud scattered into the Pennsylvania sky.

Xavier lay on the ground as if frozen to the spot. He may have remained that way if not for the sight of the soldiers marching toward him in rigid military formation. Xavier sprang to his feet and ran for Andy. The other boy looked about as if he were waking from an inescapable nightmare. His expression became even more horrified when he saw what Xavier held in his hands. He pushed himself away from Xavier and stumbled to his feet. He might have run down the gentle slope of the hill but the sight of the advancing soldiers stopped him in his tracks.

"We have to get back inside," Xavier told him. "Fast!"

Andy looked from the soldiers to the bear paw in Xavier's hands and back to the soldiers.

"Andy! Listen to me! We need to move, *now*!"

The soldiers stopped their advance no more than fifty feet from the two boys. The front row knelt, the back row remained standing. All swung their rifles from their shoulders and aimed them at the two new targets in front of them.

That got Andy moving. He took a single step toward the house. He yelped and clutched his right leg.

Xavier wasted no time. He threw Andy's arm over his shoulder and moved as quickly as the other boy's weight would allow for the broken back door of the house.

No sound came from the soldier's rifles yet Xavier could feel the musket balls whiz past his head. They chewed into the wooden slats of the house and sent plumes of dirt and grass into the air around them. When they reached the steps that led to the back door Xavier threw Andy across the threshold before he hurled himself after the boy. They skidded and rolled across the kitchen floor, coming to rest in front of the refrigerator.

He half-expected to see the soldiers charging into the kitchen through the open door but they had not moved since assuming their firing positions. *Maybe they* can't *come in,* the voice in Xavier's head suggested. *It's not like that old door could have stopped them before.* "Good point," Xavier replied.

His eyes were drawn to the zone of darkness that surrounded Tah-tah Kro'-ah. She hovered above the floor against the far wall of the kitchen. Carlos, Navaeh, and Maya knelt on the ancient linoleum before her. Carlos glanced over his shoulder at Xavier, his eyes pleading.

Xavier grabbed Andy's shoulders. "Try to get away from her. I'm gonna see if I can end this." Then he dashed for the basement door. He tried to conceal the giant bear paw beneath his shirt as he ran. To his surprise the raven queen did not come after him. *Oh, don't worry, she will*, the voice in his head assured him. *As soon as she's done doing whatever she's gonna do to your friends, you're next on her list*. This time Xavier did not reply.

He took the basement steps two at a time, no longer concerning himself with how they creaked their protest. When he reached the bottom he whirled and started toward the back of the basement. "That's where it has to be, right?" he asked the darkness.

The bear paw grew colder in his hands. The meager light spilling down the steps did not penetrate the far side of the basement and Xavier was quickly enveloped in darkness. "Come on, come on, where is it?"

He gasped suddenly and dropped the bear paw. It had grown so cold it was as if he were holding onto a small slab of ice. Xavier stopped, closed his eyes. It was not just the bear paw that had grown cold; the air temperature around him had plummeted suddenly and dramatically. Xavier opened his eyes and looked down.

There was nothing remarkable about the ground upon which he stood, other than the intense cold radiating from it. Xavier could feel the cold even through the soles of his sneakers. He could see nothing but he knew his breath was frosting the air.

He knelt, felt about the ground. Just as quickly he pulled his hand back. "Geez, that's cold!" He felt about for the bear paw and scooped it up. It was cold but he must be growing accustomed to it; he could tolerate the cold now where he could not a moment before. "This has to be it."

He took a long, slow breath, felt the icy air invade his lungs. This was not going to be fun. Before he could talk himself out of it, he slid his arm into the bear paw. Xavier gasped. The cold within the hollow appendage was deep and penetrated his skin and muscles in an instant. Immediately his arm went numb. The pins-and-needles sensation worked its way up his arm toward his shoulder. "Better hurry," he mumbled.

Xavier raised his arm and swung down with everything he had. The claws tore at the cold, hard ground that made up the basement floor. Frozen dirt pelted his cheeks and his neck. Xavier struck down again.

You'd better proceed with haste, a voice behind him intoned. Xavier did not need to turn to know it was Caleb Mason who spoke. *They're coming.*

"'They're?'" But he was afraid he already knew the answer.

The numbness had reached his shoulder and was continuing its march onward. Already his neck and chest began to stiffen.

On the next swipe at the floor he felt the claws brush something that wasn't dirt. He paused, then whispered, "Found you." He struck the ground again, and again he felt the claws strike something hard and unyielding. Xavier dug furiously, as fast as his numb muscles would allow. Although he could see very little he knew he had succeeded in uncovering something. And he knew what that something was. With his other hand he reached into the hole he had created and withdrew the small black idol from the ground.

If the air around him was cold the idol itself was Arctic. Xavier lost all feeling in his other hand. He yelped and dropped the idol from his numb fingers; it lay on the ground in front of him like a sleeping—but awakening— tarantula.

"Xavier, stop."

This time it was not the ghost of Caleb Mason who spoke. Xavier turned, at once knowing and dreading what he would see. His friends who had accompanied him to the house—and Kyle Reed— stood perhaps ten feet behind him. Their arms were by their sides, their blank eyes stared straight ahead. They could almost have been sleepwalking. And perhaps they were. Behind them, blotting out the light from upstairs, hovered the raven queen.

"She doesn't want to hurt us," Carlos continued. "She only wants to help us to see."

"Listen to her, Xavier," Maya added, her voice and expression as blank as Carlos's.

Xavier gulped. It took every bit of strength he had left to raise the bear claw above his head. He brought it down at the idol.

The raven queen roared and surged past the other kids. Her fingers, tendrils of frigid darkness, wrapped themselves around his wrist. Xavier gasped. The cold which had been slowly overtaking his body now flooded over him and completed the job. The world started to go black around him.

Something pulled down on his arm, a new presence that had not been there a moment before. Xavier opened one eye. Caleb Mason, along with a host of others, the Sullivan children among them, struggled against the force of the raven queen's strength. She screeched her protest at their unexpected resistance.

Caleb looked at Xavier and nodded.

Xavier pulled with everything he had left. Tah-tah-Kro'-ah's black fingers slipped a bit on his wrist. She screeched again and leaned down, her beaklike mouth inches from his face. Her eyes blazed with icy, red fire.

Xavier screamed and brought his arm down with the last of his strength. He slipped from the raven queen's grip and the bear claws raked across the idol. Tah-tah-Kro'-ah threw her head back and wailed. The sound seemed to shake the entire house. Dust drifted down from the ceiling and several ancient knickknacks tumbled from the walls and broke upon the ground.

Again, Caleb told him. He and the other ghosts seemed to be losing their struggle against the raven queen. Xavier could see them starting to fall away.

Xavier did as Caleb told him and struck the idol again. This time the raven queen spread the darkness that was her wings. The spirits flew back and faded from view. Free of them, Tah-tah-Kro'-ah collapsed to the ground. As she did, Xavier's classmates staggered and gripped the walls and each other to keep from falling.

Tah-tah-Kro'-ah pulled herself along the basement floor toward Xavier. Her eyes, ablaze with hatred, focused squarely on him. Her beaklike mouth opened and snapped shut with each inch she gained.

"It's over, Your Highness." Xavier stuck the idol a final time.

The explosion was silent. It threw Xavier into the far corner of the basement. Old junk rained down on him from the walls. He covered up as best as his frozen muscles allowed. Wind tore through the room with such intensity Xavier thought the whole house would collapse upon him.

Yet the house remained standing. The wind, for all its ferocity, died quickly. Xavier became aware that he could hear his own breathing again. The numbness that had overtaken his body vanished all at once. Slowly, afraid of what he might see, he opened his eyes.

Caleb Mason stood over him and favored him with an odd smile. He extended his hand. Xavier took it and Caleb helped him to his feet. *Thank you*, the boy soldier said.

"Don't mention it," Xavier mumbled. Then Caleb was gone and Xavier was left alone in the dark.

No, not alone. He could hear coughs and groans coming from somewhere ahead of him. His arms outstretched, Xavier moved forward. Light began to intrude into the darkness of the basement and Xavier realized he was getting close to the bottom of the steps. His friends were there, helping each other up and shaking the cobwebs from their minds.

"You guys okay?" Xavier asked.

Maya threw her arms around him and planted a single kiss on his cheek. "Thank you," she whispered.

"Eww!" Andy exclaimed, and laughed.

Navaeh slapped him gently on the back of his head. "Quiet!" She turned to Xavier. "Is that it? Is it over?"

Xavier looked about the mess caused by the silent explosion. "I guess so."

Carlos shook his hand. "Not bad, Valsaint. Of course, *I* did all the heavy lifting." He laughed as well.

There was an audible *thud* from somewhere upstairs. All of them jumped at the sound. Xavier had time to think, *Oh no. She can't be back!* Then he heard Mr.

Bisaillon's voice calling from somewhere near the kitchen. "Kids! Kids, are you in here? Are you all right?"

"Down here, Mr. B," Andy called up the stairs. "We're coming up."

Andy led the way up the steps. Kyle Reed held back until he was alone in the basement with Xavier. "Um, you gonna say anything about what I did in here?" He sounded sheepish, a tone Xavier had never heard from Kyle as long as he had known him.

"Probably. Okay, maybe not *all* of it. We'll see." Then he headed upstairs.

Mr. Bisaillon stood in the kitchen. Both girls were hugging him around his waist and both Carlos and Andy stood nearby. All sported broad smiles. Mr. Bisaillon's widened when he saw the last of his missing students emerge from the basement.

"You guys all okay?"

"More or less," Xavier replied. "How'd you get away from those soldiers?"

Mr. Bisaillon shrugged. "They just wandered off a few minutes ago. Never said a word the whole time. The ravens, too. Flew away in all directions. As soon as they left I came inside. The front door was so rotted it fell inside the house as soon as I touched it." He looked about the ruined kitchen. "What the heck happened in here?"

"It's a long story," Carlos told him.

"You got that right," Navaeh added.

"I'm just glad you guys are okay," Mr. Bisaillon told them. "Oh, Xavier, I found something that belongs to you." He reached into his back pocket and withdrew Xavier's cell phone.

Xavier gaped. "I forgot all about this!" He powered it up and was rewarded with three solid bars at the top of the display. "I think it's gonna work!" He called up his home number and hit the green button.

At first he heard nothing. For an awful moment he thought the raven queen had returned, her disappearance a cruel trick to play upon the kids before she took them all away. He even took a step toward the kitchen door, ready to run straight through it if that's what it took to get out of the house. He looked into the eyes of everyone in the kitchen. They stared back at him. No one breathed.

Then he heard the familiar ringtone and after a moment, his mother's voice. "Xavier? Xavier, where are you?"

He released a breath he was unaware he held and smiled broadly. His companions started breathing again. Carlos and Andy slapped each other's hands.

"Mom, there's no way you're gonna believe me, so here's Mr. Bisaillon. He'll explain the whole thing."

"Honey, wait! What—"

Xavier offered the phone to his teacher. Mr. Bisaillon ruffled Xavier's hair and took the phone. As he began to speak to the woman on the other end, Xavier looked at his friends.

"Let's get the hell outta here."

Amid nods of agreement and some relieved laughter, they headed for the front door.

About the Author

Joe grew up in Connecticut's Naugatuck Valley. A voracious reader since he was old enough to hold a book in his hands, he surprised his second-grade teacher by using the word "invulnerable" (learned from a Superman comic book) in a sentence.

He wrote his first story at the ripe old age of 11. His published works include the novels *The Last Battleship* and *Mon Dust*.

His favorite authors and influences include such authors as Richard Matheson, Rod Sterling, Agatha Christie, Stephen King, Alan Moore and Neil Gaiman.

Tell-Tale Publishing would like to thank you for your purchase. If you would like to read other works by this or other fine TT authors, please visit our website:

www.tell-talepublishing.com

***